Murder With a Fudge Brownie to Go

An Ivy Clark Mystery

Kristy T Dixon

Book Cover by Mariah Sinclair

Edited by Jenny Sim edition [Year of Publication]

1st edition 2024

ISBN 978-1-960841-26-1 Paperback

ISBN 978-1-960841-27-8 ebook

ISBN 978-1-960841-29-2 Hardback

To the Davis County Librarians. Thanks for taking the time to share your knowledge.

Chapter 1

This was it. I was going to die. Funny, I never pictured it happening like this. The world flew by me as I sped down a hill on Boyd's electric bike. Why had I let him talk me into this? I was going way too fast, and I was not in control. The dirt road wasn't as smooth as it could be, and I felt my teeth knocking together as I bumped over the uneven ground. I could hear Boyd yelling something behind me, but I couldn't focus on his words.

There was no way I would be able to stop while I was on the hill, so I concentrated on staying upright. The bike handles were firmly in my grip, and it took everything in me to keep going forward and not tip. If I survived this, Boyd was going to be sorry. If I didn't, I would come back and haunt him. I'd told him more than once that I didn't want to ride this thing, but he'd persisted.

The hill ended, and I continued rocketing down the road. My brain had forgotten how to stop. How did Boyd control this monster? Starting on a hill had been a bad idea. What had Boyd been thinking? My head and hand finally communicated, and I pulled on one brake and then the other. I made sure not to do it too fast, and I came to a gradual stop.

I got off the bike and glared up the hill. Boyd was strolling toward me. Taking off the green helmet, I tossed it to the side and placed a hand on my racing heart. I focused on breathing at a regular speed. Normally, I would grab the bike and meet Boyd, but I was too busy trying to get my shaking body under control.

"Wow, Ivy! You were really flying!" Boyd called as he got closer.

"And I almost died!"

He stopped in front of me and grinned. "I watched the entire thing, and you did well enough."

I pushed a stray lock of blond hair behind my ear. "Why did we start on a hill? I'm never getting on one of those things again. You probably shouldn't either. It's dangerous!"

He chuckled. "It's the greatest mode of transportation I've been on in my entire seventy years. It beats a regular bike any day. You need to give it another chance."

"Not today. I need to go change and help at the diner. José is training some new people, and he might need me."

It wasn't exactly a lie. José was training new people, and he might need me, but it wasn't likely. José had my diner running like a well-oiled machine. Promoting him to the manager was the best decision I'd ever made, and it had only been three weeks.

"If you don't try again soon, it will be too late. It could snow any day. Do you want a ride back to your car?" Boyd asked.

"No way," I said, starting toward my car. "Do you want a ride back to town?"

"No, I'll take my bike." He picked up his helmet and strapped it over his mostly bald head. "I'll see you at the diner later today." He climbed on his bike and rode off like it was the easiest thing in the world. He went up the hill like a pro. I'd been outdone by a guy at least forty years older than me.

I walked up the hill and sighed. I was wasting time. Construction would begin any day on my diner, and I should be there when the contractor comes. He hadn't given me a firm date, but I was hopeful. Expanding Sue's Diner would be glorious.

I smiled as I thought about the expansion. We would be able to fit twice as many people at the tables, and my dwelling above the diner would be more than a room and bathroom. It would be like an actual apartment. Creepers was going to love it. My cat loved to stay in my room by the window, but I wanted to give him more room to explore during the day.

My legs burned from the walk up, and I realized I'd made a mistake when I stopped teaching Zumba. I was getting weak. After the expansion of the diner was complete, I would start it up again. A bunch of older town citizens had taken the class, and we'd had a good time.

I climbed into my gray Kia Soul and started down the road. A picture of my library book popped into my head, and my mouth turned down. I'd been trying to ignore it, but I couldn't. In the back of the book, someone had written "I know who killed Tabitha, and I'll take it to my grave." It had to be a joke, but what if it wasn't?

Most of the books in the Muddy Creek library were donated. It wasn't run by the city or the state; it was run by Brian Hooper. The book could have come from anywhere. In the front of the book, it said S. Roberts. I'd been itching to find out who S. Roberts and Tabitha were, but things had been hectic since a crazy harvest festival had brought about a dead body. Now that it was over, I felt nervous about pulling up another mystery.

I loved a good mystery, and I'd solved two since moving to Muddy Creek, Kansas, this past summer, but I should probably take a break. I kept saying this to myself, but I was sure I'd be trying to figure out who Tabitha was by tomorrow. It was nagging at me way too much.

I drove into town and past the businesses on the square. There aren't a lot, but this is where everyone comes to buy things. I pulled up to the brick diner and parked. My gramma had started this diner, and now it was mine. I smiled at the Sue's Diner sign and unlocked the door. The cooks had already come in this morning, but they entered through the back. I could hear them in the kitchen.

Creepers would be waiting for his breakfast, so I crossed the diner and went upstairs to my room. Creepers was sleeping on my pillow when I opened the door. I grabbed a can of cat food and popped the top. His head came up, and he yawned.

"Are you hungry?" I asked, dumping the food into his bowl.

He stretched and jumped to the floor. He rubbed his soft gray head against my jeans, then went to his dish. I smelled like cold air and sweat, so I took a quick shower and put on a fresh change of clothing. I'm excited for snow but nervous about being cold. This will be my first winter that isn't in Arizona, and I'm prepared to freeze.

I got ready as quickly as I could and started for the door. I paused and glanced over at the library copy of *Jane Eyre* and frowned. I picked it up and flipped to the back. "I know who killed Tabitha. Ugh, Creepers, I can't leave this alone."

He ignored me and kept chewing. I tossed the book to the bed and went to the kitchen. José was telling the new cooks the importance of covering their hair while cooking. His black hair was slicked back and covered by a hairnet. Anton stirred something and mumbled to himself. He had only worked here for a few weeks, but he's a fast learner. He's twenty-five and still deciding what he wanted to do with his life. Anton was originally from Brooklyn and had only lived in Muddy Creek for a few years.

"Do you need me?" I asked José.

He glanced over at me. "I think we're good unless you want to make some brownies. We might have enough for today, but it will be close."

"I can do that." Baking is my passion. I'm not big on the rest of the cooking, but desserts are my thing. I grabbed my hideous neon cat apron and pulled it over my head. The sheriff gave it to me, and I only wear it when I think he might come in. I took a mixing bowl and started gathering ingredients.

"Have you had breakfast?" José asked me. "I heard you come in earlier."

I rolled my eyes. "No, I haven't. I let Boyd talk me into riding his bike. I'm amazed I'm still alive."

José laughed. "Boyd loves that bike."

"He had me start on a hill! I was sure I was going to fall off."

"I'm thinking of getting one. He let me ride it the other day, and it was pretty fun. I'll wait until spring, though."

"I thought it was terrifying." I grinned mischievously. "Maybe it's an old guy thing."

Anton and the other two cooks laughed.

"Hey, you shouldn't be making fun of us old guys," José said. "I rode that thing around like a pro."

I just smiled. José wasn't that old. I'd put him at about fifty and in much better shape than most people I knew. He's a runner and still does marathons at least once a year. He's one of the younger friends I'd met in Muddy Creek. It's a small farming town and getting smaller all the time.

"I'll stick to driving," I said. "I might be getting too old for those kinds of thrills."

Anton grinned. "What are you, twenty-eight?"

"Twenty-nine and getting closer to that other number I don't want to say out loud." Getting older didn't actually bother me, but thirty sounded a lot older than twenty-nine.

The back door opened, and Livy came in. She grabbed a purple apron and pulled it over her long red hair. "Hey, everyone."

José glanced at her. "Hi, Liv. Can you unlock the front door?"

"Sure," she said, leaving the kitchen. Livy was starting college in January, so we were going to lose her. Most of our servers were in high school, so it would be rough when she left. A good portion of the adults around here had farms and no time to work in diners.

"Next week is Thanksgiving," I said, dumping chocolate powder in my bowl. "No one is going to come to the diner that day, are they?"

José shook his head. "When Linda owned the diner, we closed on Thanksgiving." My aunt Linda owned the diner after my grandma.

"So no one would come?" I didn't want to be alone on Thanksgiving. With my parents in Arizona, it would be a sad day.

José tilted his head. "I bet some would. A lot of older single people might. I don't mind coming in and cooking. I don't have any family around."

"What if we spread the word that a reservation is needed? Then we would know what to expect, and if no one wants to come, we won't bother."

"I'd love to make a Thanksgiving feast," José said. "Even if one person wants to come, I'm willing. Besides, you need a good meal that day, and I know you'll eat a frozen burrito if I don't make it."

I stirred the brownies and glared at him. "I can cook something that isn't in the microwave."

He laughed. "I'm sure Boyd will want to come."

"Alright, let's do it." I went to the fridge and grabbed a zucchini. My zucchini brownies were amazing. I grabbed my vegetable peeler and went to work. Even if it was only José, Boyd, and me, it would be worth it.

José went back to helping the new cooks. They were both women around forty. I think they are sisters because I'd seen them together at the diner a few times, and they had a similar look. Their applications had different last names, but they could be married.

"Hey, so do any of you know of a person named Tabitha?" I couldn't help it. It slipped out. The kitchen went quiet, and I looked up from my zucchini. The two women were staring at me with their brows furrowed. José's lips were pursed, and he shook his head and put a quick finger to his lips. Anton looked indifferent.

"I just thought it might be a good name for another cat someday," I said, trying to backpedal. "I just wouldn't want to name a cat something someone else was named." It sounded lame even to me.

One woman bit her lip. "I wouldn't name a cat Tabitha," she said. "Everyone around here would avoid the poor thing."

"Noted. How about Sheila?" I said, trying to remove the tension.

The woman let out a slow breath. "That would be better."

"Good to know." I wasn't really planning on getting another cat, and now I was more curious than ever. Who was Tabitha, and who killed her?

Chapter 2

"I smell brownies," Sheriff Jett Malone said, entering the kitchen. Jett and Boyd were the only people not on staff who came into the kitchen whenever they felt like it.

"They're still in the oven," I told him. "It will be at least twenty more minutes, and then they have to cool. Besides, it's still breakfast time."

He flashed his gorgeous grin, and my stomach fluttered. "I suppose."

José turned to Anton. "Hey, Anton, can you keep an eye on things for a minute? I need to talk to the sheriff."

Anton nodded. "Sure, boss."

José headed for the back door with Jett at his heels. "You can come too, Ivy."

I followed, wondering if this had something to do with Tabitha. I walked into the frigid fall air and shivered.

José closed the door and turned to Jett. "Ivy was just asking about Tabitha."

Jett's mouth turned down. "Where did you hear about her?"

I shrugged. "Who is she?"

"She was a woman who used to live around here. About ten years ago, she drowned."

My eyes narrowed. "So it was an accident?"

"No one saw it. It happened in the middle of the night, and no one knew about it until morning."

I rubbed my lips together. If no one saw it...

Jett groaned. "I know that look, Miss Ivy Clark. You are going to say this is a murder and then have us all wrapped up in it."

José shook his head. "There should be a rule that we can only solve murders if they are at least a month apart. I haven't recovered from the last one." He said that, but his eyes were sparkling.

"Both of you come up to my room. I need to show you something." They followed me through the diner and upstairs. "I would tell you to sit, but I don't have any great places to sit at the moment."

Jett looked around. "Your room looks much better than the last time I saw it. At least you have a bed now."

When I first came here, I'd been sleeping on the floor, but now I'd turned the dirty little room into a cute little place of solitude. I grabbed the library book from my bed and opened it to the last page. "Look at this."

Jett took the book and read the writing. His eyes narrowed, and his frown deepened. He handed it to José.

"What do you think?" I asked, wringing my hands.

Jett ran a hand through his short brown hair. "I don't know. It could be a prank. Everyone in town knows about Tabitha."

"Was she alone by the water? What happened?"

"I don't know the exact details," Jett said. "I wasn't the sheriff back then, but I remember when it happened. Muddy Creek is a tight community, and the town used to do a yearly retreat. A lot of people would participate. One year, they rented big houseboats and met at a lake. In the morning, Tabitha was gone. They found her body a day later."

I frowned. "That's awful."

José closed the book. "You'll have a hard time finding anybody to agree with you."

I raised my brow. "Oh?"

"You saw how Carrie and Tiffany reacted when you mentioned her name."

"The new cooks?"

"Yes," José said. "Tabitha got a bunch of people in town to invest in a pyramid scheme. People around here trust each other, so it wasn't hard to get participants. She promised them they would make money. It all fell apart, and everyone lost tons of money."

Jett nodded. "It wasn't a fun year for Muddy Creek."

José leaned down to pick up Creepers, who was nuzzling his shoe. "No, it wasn't. Tiffany's and Carrie's families lost a ton. That's probably why they're working here. Some people never completely recovered. Those two have been doing odd jobs for years to get their savings up to where it was."

"She probably didn't do it on purpose," I said. "Lots of people lose money in pyramid schemes."

Jett shrugged. "Tabitha said she lost money, but you wouldn't know it to see her. She was spending money left and right. Some people believed she actually took all the money, then pretended it was all lost."

José ran his hand over Creepers's back. "More than a few people. When she died, people thought it might be foul play, but no one cared much. Everyone was still really mad and thought she deserved it."

"Interesting. How many people were on the boat?"

Jett scratched the stubble on his chin. "If I remember right, twelve."

"Yep, twelve," José agreed. "I remember when they were talking about it. Not many people were at the retreat that year, and they all fit on four houseboats."

"Were either of you there?"

They both shook their heads.

"Was there an investigation?"

Jett crossed his arms and looked at the ceiling. "Let me think. There must have been. I know they questioned everyone there, but nothing ever came from it. At least not that I know of."

"Someone must have seen it," I said, picking up the book, "or they wouldn't have written it in here."

Jett gave me the look he gets when he doesn't want to tell me my theory is flawed. He put a hand on my shoulder. "Any teenager could have written that as a joke. I can even see some adults who might think they're funny."

"Wait, there's a name." I flipped to the front of the book and pointed at the faded blue ink. "S. Roberts. It's the same handwriting."

José looked at Jett, his eyebrow arched. "You don't suppose it's Stan Roberts?"

Jett nodded. "It sounds like him. He was the only Roberts I know of around here."

"Was?" I asked.

Jett sat at the foot of my bed and rested his elbows on his knees. "He died a year or two after Tabitha."

"Who was he?"

José grinned. "A character, that's for sure. He was around sixty-five. There were these treasure hunts he would put on for the harvest festivals. He would hide a treasure chest full of gems somewhere in or around Muddy Creek. There were clues, and all the town would go wild trying to find it."

"Was it worth a lot?"

"Not really. The gems were pretty, but they weren't diamonds or anything. The chest probably added up to around three hundred dollars. Nothing to lose your mind over."

"I'd almost bet it was him," Jett said. "He was always making up competitions."

"What happened to him?" I asked.

Jett's eyes widened. "It was really weird. He disappeared not too long after Tabitha died. No one knew where he was. A year later, a new grave appeared in the cemetery with his name on it. People have speculated, but no one knows what happened."

"Who is in charge of the cemetery?"

Jett shrugged. "Someone in Wichita. It's a mess. People care for their own relatives' graves or they get overgrown. There's no budget for it."

"With Stan being dead, that is going to make things difficult," I said, already feeling overwhelmed.

Jett looked up at me and frowned. "This one is over your head, Ivy. Without Stan, no one is going to figure it out. Stan had a sense of humor as well. He might have done it to be funny."

I crossed my arms. "That's a sad sense of humor."

"I'm just saying, even if Stan knew something, he's dead, so what do you have to go on?"

"I don't know, but I have to try. I've been trying to ignore it for weeks and it's been driving me mad."

Jett let out a slow breath. "So I have to say it?"

I grinned. "You want me to take José or Boyd if I go snooping?"

He gave me a tired smile. "Yes."

José smiled. "I'm up for it."

I looked at José's apron and pointed above Creepers. "You better change your apron. Creepers has been shedding up a storm this week."

"Oh man," he said, putting Cosmic Creepers on my bed. "I can't believe you let him sleep on your bed."

"I have to change my pillowcase every day. He rarely sheds, but I haven't brushed him enough in the past few weeks."

"So what's our plan?" José asked.

"We go to the cemetery tomorrow. It did say he would take the secret to his grave."

Jett stood and went to the door. "It's supposed to snow tomorrow, so plan for that. I'm going down to get some breakfast."

I turned to José. "Maybe we should go tonight? It will be dark after you get off, though."

“We could wait until tomorrow and deal with snow. Snow might be easier than the dark. Your brownies are probably burning.”

“Oh no!” I hurried down the stairs, through the dining area, and into the kitchen. The brownies were sitting on the island, cooling.

Anton turned from the eggs he was scrambling. “I took the brownies out.”

“Thank you!” I said, turning off the oven. I wondered how many pans of brownies I would have to make to get my mind off Tabitha.

Chapter 3

The following morning, I sat on my window seat, staring out at the white world. I'd seen snow before, but only once. Creepers slept on my lap, and I held a cup of hot chocolate. I'd finally gotten a coat, boots, and gloves, and I couldn't wait to wear them. I was meeting José in a few minutes, and we hoped to be finished at the cemetery before the diner opened.

The doorbell rang, and I transferred Creepers to his bed on the windowsill. I slipped my boots over my fuzzy socks and pulled on my gloves and my cute purple coat. On the way downstairs, I slid my hood over my hair. José and Boyd peeked through the glass door. It was still dark outside.

"Hey," I said, going out and locking the door behind me. Boyd's face was covered in a scarf, with only his eyes poking out. José wore a jacket, but he seemed comfortable.

"Good morning," José said. "Are you ready for this?"

"Totally ready." The snow was less than an inch deep, and I loved the crunch under my boots. If we didn't have somewhere to be, I would walk around the square just to hear it. We walked to my car, and I stopped, staring at the snow-covered car. "How do I get the snow off so I can see?" I wiped some away with my glove.

José and Boyd both laughed. "Don't you have a snow brush?" José asked.

"A what?"

Boyd's eyes danced. "I'm not sure I want to risk my life in a car with someone who doesn't know what a snow scraper is."

José chuckled. "I was thinking the same thing. I'll drive."

We walked over to José's car. The windows were already clear. I climbed into the front seat and noticed something resembling a humongous toothbrush. Snow melted from the bristles and onto the floorboard.

I pointed at it. "Snow brush?"

"Yep," José said, starting the car. "You need to get one if you're going to drive around here. You can get one at Hal's, or I think the grocery store carries some."

I put that information on my mental checklist. I stared out the window in awe as the snow-covered world went past. Small flakes continued to fall.

"You look impressed, Ivy," Boyd said.

I grinned. "All the Christmas songs finally make sense. It's so pretty."

Once we were out of town, José surprised me by staying on the road. No one had driven out here since the snow had started, so I couldn't see any sign of the road. For all I knew, he was driving through a field. The snow seemed to go on forever.

After ten minutes, we drove past a rusty gate and under an old sign that said Muddy Creek Cemetery. I was really glad not to be the one driving. I probably would have run off the road and gotten lost. José parked the car, and I unbuckled my seat belt and climbed out.

I looked up at the flurries and smiled. I wanted to stick out my arms and spin, but José and Boyd would surely tease me.

"Do you know where Stan's grave is?" I asked. The cemetery wasn't huge, but it would be hard to find the right one if they didn't know where it was.

"I have no idea," Boyd said. "I've never seen it."

José rubbed his chin. "I saw it once, but it was a long time ago. Everyone was coming to look since it popped out of nowhere. I think it was over in the southeast corner somewhere."

We walked through the fresh powder and started scanning the graves. They had a small sprinkling of snow, but it didn't cover the words on the upright ones.

"Do you remember what it looked like?" I asked.

José frowned. "I know it wasn't flat. I really can't remember anything else."

The sun was rising, but it was still hard to see the writing. I pulled out my phone and turned on the flashlight. I shined it over the graves, ignoring the flat ones.

My light stopped on one in the shape of a heart. "Tabitha Lynell Coats." José and Boyd stared at it with me. I did the math. "She was only twenty-five?"

José nodded. "That sounds about right. She went to school with Jett, but she was a few years older than him."

"How old is Jett?" I asked. Not that it mattered, but I had wondered.

"I don't know exactly. Thirty-three?"

Boyd nodded. "Something like that."

"Are Tabitha's parents still around?"

José shook his head. "They moved before she died. They couldn't handle all the people who were upset about getting ripped off by Tabitha."

"But she didn't care?"

"Not really. She didn't even pretend to act apologetic. Tabitha was always really into herself. I think she figured people would eventually move on and accept her again."

"I wonder if we can get a list of the people who were on the boat when she died."

José shrugged. "Probably. There have to be people who know. Most of them are probably still in town."

Boyd wandered away, studying the tombstones.

"Can you remember anyone who was on the boat?"

"Carrie Wilson was there," José said. "So was Greg Orwell and Cindy Baker. Those are the only three I can remember off the top of my head."

"So one of our new cooks could be a murderer?"

"I don't think Carrie is the type."

"Hey, guys! Over here!" Boyd called. We rushed over to the spot where he stood with his light shining on a large tombstone.

I squatted down and looked at it. There was a book carved on the granite above the inscription. "Stanley Bensen Roberts," I read. "Born 1452, died 1519. Son of Robert Brown. Anchiano, Italy. Well, this isn't the right guy. Those dates are way off."

"Let me see," José said, crouching down next to me. "That's odd. It has to be him. This cemetery hasn't been around long enough for those dates."

I snapped a picture with my phone. "He might be trying to tell us something. If he was using clues, there might be something we don't understand." I walked around the back but found nothing but smooth granite.

"Stan's father's name was Hubert Roberts," Boyd said. "Not Robert Brown. Stan and I both grew up in Muddy Creek, and we were only a few years apart."

"Stanley Roberts isn't an uncommon-sounding name," I said. "What if it's a different one?"

José moved his jaw from side to side. "I don't know. I remember when this grave appeared. It caused such a big stir. Plus, look at it. It's not hundreds of years old."

Boyd rubbed snow off the top of the grave. "And Stanley's middle name was probably Bensen because that was his grandparents' name. I knew them when I was young."

"Hmm," I said. "I'm getting nothing. Maybe the dates are significant. Perhaps it's the clue Stan was pointing us to when he wrote in the book."

"I guess it's possible," José said. He glanced at his watch. "We need to go if we want to get to the diner before it opens. Anton is pretty good, but he's still new."

I nodded. I had my picture. As I turned to go to the car, I saw a dark figure dart behind a tree and then run. "Look!" I pointed. They both turned and squinted into the trees.

"What?" José asked.

"I saw someone watching us."

Boyd took a step forward. "Why? No one would know what we're up to."

"Are you sure you saw someone?" José asked. "There aren't any other tire tracks, and there isn't anything else over here."

"Give me a minute. I'm going to go see if there are footprints."

José grabbed my elbow. "No way. You aren't going to run into what might be danger. I'll go."

"I should go," Boyd said. "I could drop dead any day now, anyhow."

"I'm going," I said, jogging toward the trees. José was at my side, and Boyd stood behind us with his hands on his hips.

We stopped when we got to the tree and crept around it.

"Footprints," I said, pointing at the ground. I pulled out my phone and snapped a picture.

"Let's get out of here. It's probably nothing, but if it is, it could be dangerous."

We returned to Boyd because I knew José was right. If it was someone who had nothing to do with Tabitha, then it didn't matter who they were. If they were more sinister, we weren't prepared to fight. And what were the chances anyone knew what we were here for? It was a ten-year-old mystery no one talked about.

"Did you see anything?" Boyd asked when we got to him.

"There were footprints, so it at least proves I'm not crazy," I said. "It's so cold; we should go."

On the drive home, I pulled up the picture of the tomb and frowned. I couldn't figure out any reason Stan would put the information he did on there unless it was a clue.

"If everyone was coming to look at the grave, why didn't anyone notice the strange information?" I asked.

"I guess no one looks close at that stuff," Boyd said.

I grabbed my phone and searched for Stanley Roberts and his father's name, Robert Brown. There was something about a basketball player and a few obituaries, but nothing helpful. I looked up Stanley Bensen Roberts and got information about a farmer from Muddy Creek. There wasn't anything to go off, though. I typed in Anchiano, Italy. That brought up more information than I would ever know what to do with.

"Any luck?" José asked.

"No. I'm looking at a city in Italy. I don't see that it will get me anywhere. It has a lot on the population and things to see there. It was the birthplace of Leonardo Da Vinci. That's what most of the search results are about."

Boyd leaned forward from the back seat. "Try searching for the dates."

I put 1452-1519 in the search bar. It came up with a calculator that said the answer was negative sixty-seven. Not what I wanted. I scrolled down further and gasped. "Leonardo Da Vinci was born in 1452, and he died in 1519."

Chapter 4

The cheesecake looked amazing, if I say so myself. We'd never served cheesecake at the diner, but we were experimenting to see if people liked it. I'd only ever made it twice, but it came together beautifully, thanks to hours of watching people do it on the internet. I grabbed some raspberry syrup, drizzled it over the cheesecake in a zigzag, and then placed three raspberries on top.

This deserved a picture and a social media post. I snapped a photo with my phone and took a short video. I'd thought about hiring a social media person, but, in reality, most of Muddy Creek didn't seem to be on most socials. There were potential customers from surrounding towns, but it wouldn't be worth paying someone to advertise to them.

"Wow, fancy," José said, leaning over to look. "We're really turning Sue's back into what it was when your grandma was here."

I smiled. I had such wonderful memories of my gramma Sue and the diner. When my aunt took over, she'd lost most of the magic, but we were slowly returning it. "We need to bring back the milkshakes. One of my favorite memories was sitting at the counter with a huge chocolate milkshake."

"That sounds good."

"I just worry about doing too much in such a small town. If we have too many options and not enough people, it might make it harder to know what to keep in stock."

He grinned. "That's why you hired me to be the manager. That kind of thing doesn't stress me, and I'm good at it."

"I'm glad because that is exactly what stresses me."

Creepers came tearing past my feet, and I hurried after him. Even though people were okay with cats running around the diner, I didn't want him in the kitchen. I scooped him up, and he squirmed. I carried him up to my room and gave him a treat. He gobbled it down, climbed into his favorite window, and yawned.

I grabbed the *Jane Eyre* book and sighed. "What is Stan Roberts trying to tell me?" Creepers looked out the window, ignoring me. I couldn't figure out how Leonardo Da Vinci could be connected to Tabitha. I'd flipped through every page to find anything that might help me, but I'd finally decided there wasn't anything else.

I looked at the picture of the tomb again and stared at it. There was the book engraved on top. Perhaps there was another clue in a book about Leonardo Da Vinci. What were the chances it was still in Brian's library? If all this stuff had been waiting for someone for nine or ten years, anything could have happened.

"I'm going to the library. Do you want to come?" Creepers just looked at me. "Don't you want to see Brian? And your mom?" He buried his face in his warm bed. "Well, I'm going to take you anyway because I think you would want to go if you knew what I was talking about." I pulled on my boots and coat, then grabbed Creepers and the library book.

It was cold outside, but it wasn't snowing. I walked the short distance to the library and pulled open the heavy door. Creepers jumped to the floor and took off. He'd spent the first few months of his life coming to the library with Brian.

"Hey," Brian said from behind the desk. Creepers jetted past him and disappeared into the children's section. He chuckled. "He didn't even stop to say hello. I guess he wants to get the warm spot by the window. His mom is probably already there."

"I had to force him to leave the diner. I think he's tired."

"You finished *Jane Eyre*? That's one of my favorites."

I walked over to the tall desk and put the book in front of him. I opened it to the back and showed him Stan's message. "Have you ever seen this before?"

His smile slipped as he read it. "No, I haven't. It's probably a prank."

"That's what I thought at first." I flipped to the front page. "It was donated by Stan Roberts."

He rubbed a hand over his curly black hair. "Stan Roberts is before your time here. I take it you've already been looking into this?" He turned to his computer and started typing.

"Yep. I went with José and Boyd to Stan's grave."

He looked up and arched his brow. "Oh?"

"The inscription on the grave didn't make sense. Let me find the picture."

Brian looked back at his screen. "*Jane Eyre* hasn't been checked out in years."

"Don't libraries usually get rid of books that no one checks out?"

"Usually, but I don't. I might someday, but I don't see a reason if there's room on the shelves."

I handed him my phone and watched him study the grave.

"Interesting. Born in 1452 and died in 1519. Those are the dates that Leonardo Da Vinci was alive. And he was born in Anchiano."

"You know that off the top of your head? I had to search it."

He grinned. "I have a degree in history as well as library science. I'm a bit of a nerd. I've spent my entire forty-five years reading things most people don't care about. Okay, that might be an exaggeration. I didn't learn to read until I was four."

"We should have taken you with us. It would have saved us some time. I'm wondering if he was trying to tell us that there is another clue in a book about Leonardo Da Vinci. If you never get rid of books, it must still be here."

Brian turned back to his computer. "I don't get rid of books that aren't circulated, but books get ruined or never get returned. No books in the system are only about Da Vinci. I have one about a bunch of artists from that era." He looked back at my phone. "Stan's father wasn't named Robert Brown."

"That's what Boyd said."

He rubbed his chin as he stared down, and a smile broke out across his face. "*The Da Vinci Code.*"

"What about it? Do you think that was the book he meant?"

"Dan Brown wrote the book, and Robert was the protagonist."

My eyes widened. "He mixed their names."

"It sounds like Stan. He was always making puzzles and competitions. I can't believe he would do it about something as important as this."

"Is the book in the library?"

He typed some more. "No. It looks like it got lost, and I never replaced it. It didn't get checked out a lot, and since most of my books are donated, it limits the collection."

I blew out a frustrated breath. "If we can't find it, we can't move on. Unless other books have clues in them. Have you ever seen writing in any of them?"

"Sure. When you get donated books, you get all sorts of markings. I've never seen any that made me think anything was odd about them." He looked at the computer screen. "The last person who checked it out was Barbra Todd."

My excitement picked up. "She might still have it. When did she check it out?"

"Two years ago. Barbra loses books all the time. She sometimes goes to the libraries in Wichita and has been known to return books to the wrong library. I would take her library card, but she donates more books than she loses."

"Wouldn't the libraries contact you and let you know they had your books?"

"I don't stamp the name of the library in the books. It always seemed pointless since this is the only library in town. Perhaps I should buy a stamp and hire someone to stamp all of them. It would take a while."

"Barbra comes into the diner every other day. She wasn't there yesterday, so I'll ask her about it today." I glanced around the library. Considering it was almost all donated, it was impressive. The shelves were all carved with flowers and leaves on the tops, and they were tall. "I wonder how long it would take to go through all the books to see if I can find anything."

"A long time. I bet José and Boyd would help. I will too."

"Let's not do that until I talk to Barbra. If she has the book, that would save us time. Unless the clue is too difficult to figure out. I better get going."

We walked over to Creepers's favorite window and found him cuddled up with Brian's cat, sleeping.

"Just leave him there," Brian said. "I'll bring him to you after I close."

"Alright, thanks."

Back at the diner, I found Barbra sitting in a booth with her best friend Opal. Barbra's bright blue hair stood out, as did her animated expressions. She waved her arms while she spoke. Opal shook her head. It surprised me to watch the two friends together. Barbra exuded happiness and enthusiasm, and Opal always wore a frown.

I went to their booth, and they looked over at me.

"The cheesecake is delicious," Barbra said. "I hope it stays on the menu."

I smiled. "I'm glad you like it. Can I talk to you for a minute?"

"Sure thing," Barbra said. Opal scooted in while poking her cheesecake with a fork and glaring at it. I sat next to her.

"I'm getting too old for this type of food," Opal said. "I'm going to go home with a stomach ache."

Opal always complains about the dessert, but she always orders it.

"What did you want to talk about?" Barbra asked.

"This is going to sound weird. You borrowed a book from the library two years ago and never returned it."

Barbra threw her head back and laughed. "I lose at least one a month. You're good at solving mysteries, so Brian sent you out after me? There has to be something more important than a missing library book."

Opal pointed her fork at Barbra. "I told you it would catch up to you someday."

I giggled. "That's not why I'm talking to you. The book might have something in it that I need to see. I'm working on a case, and I believe there is a clue in that copy of the book."

Barbra folded her arms on top of the table. "Well, that sounds intriguing. What was the book?"

"*The Da Vinci Code.*"

"Hmm. I remember that vaguely. My kids told me to read it, but I couldn't get into it."

"I didn't know you had kids," I said.

"I have five. They all moved out of Muddy Creek the second they were old enough."

Opal nodded. "That's the way it goes. Kids don't want to farm; they want to go to the city. All three of mine are in Wichita."

I felt like such an awful friend. I'd been here for months and didn't know either of them had kids.

Barbra grinned. "I've got thirteen grandkids, and now the great-grandkids are coming."

"You should bring them in the next time they visit."

Opal snorted, and Barbra glared at her. Barbra sighed. "They don't visit me. I visit them."

"Oh, I see," I said, feeling awkward.

"The reason they don't come is the same reason I can't find your book."

"Oh?"

"I may look put together for an old lady, but my house? Oh my house."

Opal grinned. "She's the biggest pack rat I've ever seen. She doesn't let anyone but Jett and me inside."

"I'm not a pack rat," Barbra said. "I prefer the term lover of the past."

Opal snorted again. "She hasn't thrown anything away in thirty years!"

"I'm not that bad," Barbra protested. "I throw away the garbage. Well, unless I have a sentimental reason not to."

“She’s a hoarder. Pure and simple.”

Chapter 5

I stood in the middle of Barbra's living room and tried not to look shocked. She'd led me through a small pathway from the door to this room. Boxes and plastic bins lined the hall, and this room was full of them as well.

"I usually sit over in that chair and read," Barbra said, pointing at a glider. There was a path to the glider. She had a couch, but it would take a lot of creativity to figure out how to get to it from here. Not that it would help. It was covered with piles of material.

"What do you do with a book once you finish it?"

"Depends. Sometimes I toss it onto a box so I can find it later. Of course I rarely find it again."

"Is your entire house like this?"

"Unfortunately, yes. Well, except for my room. It's my beautiful pink oasis. Everywhere else is this bad or worse."

"So the book could be anywhere."

"Yep. I know it's a problem, but it snuck up on me. After my husband died, I stopped caring about what the house looked like. After a while, it was so bad I didn't know what to do. I've thought about bulldozing the whole thing and starting over, but that seems like a big undertaking."

"I could help you clean up."

Barbra laughed. "It would take ten years!"

"But if you do a little each day, it will make a difference."

She took a slow breath and shook her head. "This house isn't small, you know."

"But if you could get control of even one room, it might make you feel better. If you cleaned the hall and this room, you could have people over."

"I'm seventy-five years old. The thought of doing that makes me tired."

"I really don't mind helping. I could look for the book in the process."

Her lips moved from side to side. "I suppose it wouldn't hurt. If the book is here, it's most likely in this room."

"Can José and Boyd come help?"

Her eyes went wide. "I can't have Boyd in here! He thinks I'm the greatest thing since they put the holes in swiss cheese. I don't want him to know I'm secretly a slob."

"Well, what about José?"

"Just you."

I looked around the room and tried not to feel discouraged. I needed to find that book, and I needed to help Barbra. "We'll have to throw away a lot of stuff."

Barbra crossed her arms. "I don't know how I feel about that."

"You don't even know what you have. What good is it going to do you?"

She sighed. "I suppose you're right. When do we start?"

"How about now?"

"Alright."

"Do you have any garbage bags?"

"I have everything. The problem is finding them." She left the room.

I couldn't believe I'd volunteered for this. I opened the closest box to me. It was full of magazines from 1992. The next box had a bunch of scarves. We didn't need garbage bags; we needed a dumpster.

"Here you go," Barbra said, tossing me a box of garbage bags.

"I say we toss this box of magazines."

She frowned. "What if I want to read them?"

"When was the last time you did?"

"I don't know. I didn't know they were there."

"And you have like, fifty scarves. You only have one neck, and I've never seen you wear a scarf. I think we should take a bunch of this to the thrift store in Wichita."

Barbra wrinkled her nose. "I'm not sure this is a good idea."

"It might be better if I go through it and you go somewhere else. You probably won't miss anything if you don't know I got rid of it."

Barbra bit her lip. "I want to say no, but it would be nice to have my children able to visit again. All of my most precious things are in an upper room. I'll do that one myself."

"I'll try to come over a few times a week to help."

"Alright."

I grabbed the box of magazines and took them to my car. It would take way too many trips to get rid of all this stuff. I went back for the scarves. "Do you think Jett could help? At least so we can use his truck?"

She put her hands on her hips and pursed her lips. "Sure. He's one person I let in. I don't need to impress him. He's too young to be on my radar." Her mouth turned up. "You can't say the same thing."

I grinned. "Ha ha."

"One thing we aren't in Muddy Creek is blind, girlie, and you've got it bad for hunky Sheriff Jett."

I turned to another box so Barbra wouldn't see my cheeks turn an unnatural shade of red. "You are crazy. Jett's a good guy, but we're just friends."

"Have you kissed him yet?"

"No."

"But you plan to?"

"No!" I said, pulling open a box full of random game pieces.

"Alright, I'll let you live in denial a little longer. If you ever need advice, you know where I am."

"Advice?"

"Yep. I know how to catch a man. It's all about your style," she said, running a hand through her blue hair.

"I'm sure it is."

"Have you ever thought of dyeing your hair?"

I pulled a broken game board from the box. "I dye my hair."

She gasped and put her hand dramatically to her chest. "You aren't a natural blond?"

"Not this blond. My natural color is darker."

"Have you ever thought of pink?"

"Are you saying that if I dye my hair pink, I'll catch Jett?"

"Catch me doing what?" Jett asked, entering the room.

My eyes went wide, and Barbra laughed.

"Catch you and get you to help me," I said lamely.

"What do you need help with?"

Barbra patted my arm. "Ivy wants to find a book I lost so bad she's going to help me clean out all my priceless boxes."

"Wow, I'm proud of you, Barbra. I can help. I've offered before."

Barbra looked at me. "Jett comes over twice a week to make sure I'm not dead or anything."

I grinned. "That's nice of him."

"I'm a nice guy," Jett said. "What do you want me to do?"

"Can we load things in your truck? I think a lot of this can be donated."

"Sure. What book are we looking for?"

"*The Da Vinci Code*."

"Ah. I was at the diner earlier, and Boyd caught me up on everything. Barbra has the book?"

"I checked it out years ago and lost it. It's probably not here. I'm usually good about remembering library books, just not which library I got them from."

I handed the broken game box to Jett. "Which library would you have taken it to?"

"One in Wichita."

"There's more than one?"

"Yep. There are quite a few, but I usually go to the Alford or Rockwell branches."

Jett nodded. "I've seen the Alford building. Why don't we load up the truck, then we can take it into Wichita and visit the library?"

"Sounds good." I opened a box and wrinkled my nose. There were two dead plants and a throw pillow with a hole. We might have to go donate some and take some to the dump.

By the time the truck was full, I was sweating, even with the cool air outside. Barbra had gone upstairs so she didn't have to watch. I made sure we didn't throw out anything that might be sentimental or worth money. We started making a pile of things that could be used in a yard sale.

I climbed into Jett's truck and hoped I didn't smell. My vanilla body wash might not have the power to overwhelm the smell of sweat. Jett got in, and we drove away from Barbra's house.

"This is a big job you've taken on," Jett said. "It's going to take forever."

"I know, but I need to find that book, and Barbra really needs to get her house back."

"That's true. I'm glad she agreed. For years, I've told her she shouldn't be living in that mess." He grinned and looked sideways at me. "So what were you saying when I came in the house?"

I looked out the side window. "I don't know what you're talking about."

"Something about using pink hair to catch me."

I gave a small fake laugh. "That was all Barbra. You know how she is."

He chuckled. "I do indeed. And just so you know, you don't need pink hair to catch my attention. You caught it when you first moved here."

Chapter 6

The Alford Library was a long brown building with a roof that almost looked like it was melting off. It hung lower on one side and had large glass windows in the front. We walked through the glass doors and up to a middle-aged woman with brown hair and a bright green shirt. We didn't have time to wander around aimlessly.

The librarian smiled. "Can I help you?"

"I'm Sheriff Jett Malone from Muddy Creek. Do you have a minute to answer a few questions?" Jett shook her hand.

The woman's smile fell. "Of course. What can I do for you?"

Jett turned to me, and I stepped forward. "If a person were to return a book to the library that didn't come from the library, what would happen to it?"

"Hmm..." She looked up at the ceiling in thought. "Well, we would put it in a drawer, and if no one ever claimed it, we would either put it into circulation, sell it, or throw it away. It depends on the condition and the demand for the book type."

"Do you have any copies of *The Da Vinci Code*?" Jett asked.

"Yes, I'm pretty sure we have a few. Do you want me to find a copy for you?"

"Can we see all the available copies?"

She shrugged. "I don't see why not. Did you accidentally return one?"

I shook my head. "We didn't, but a friend did. It was two years ago. The book might have a clue to an unsolved case."

"That's a long time," she said, raising her brow and typing into her computer. "We have three available at this library and eight copies at other libraries. Follow me, and I'll take you to them."

She led us past a few shelves and down an aisle. She pointed at three copies of the book. "Is there anything else I can help you with?"

"We'll let you know," Jett said. She smiled and walked away.

Jett grabbed a copy, and I picked up another. I was trying to forget about what Jett had said in the truck. Jett made my heart beat out of control, but instead of saying anything about his revelation, I'd changed the subject and stayed on safe topics for the rest of the drive. I'd never been good about these kinds of things... and what if he'd been joking?

I flipped to the back of the book. Nothing. I looked at the first page. Still nothing. I grabbed the other book and didn't see anything.

Jett snapped the book shut. "There's nothing here."

"I didn't find anything in these either. Should we go to the other library?"

"Yeah, but I'll check these out, just in case."

I nodded, and we took them up to the desk.

Jett pushed the books over to the librarian and handed her his library card.

She smiled, but looked concerned. "You want to check them all out?"

Jett shrugged. "We need to take time to search through them carefully. Don't worry, we'll bring them back."

"Are you going to any of the other libraries?" she asked as she scanned his card.

"The Rockwell branch."

"I'll call them and ask them to have any copies they have ready for you at the desk."

"Thank you. That's very kind."

"I'm always happy to help."

We made our way over to the Rockwell Library. While Jett drove, I flipped slowly through all the pages. Nothing looked out of the ordinary. "I hope they didn't sell it or throw it away."

"Me too. Oh, and I forgot to tell you. I found the file about Tabitha."

"Oh?" I asked, getting excited. "Was there anything helpful?"

"The case was handled by a different city because the lake wasn't in Muddy Creek's jurisdiction. I called the police chief there, and he faxed me everything from the file. There wasn't a lot. All the people on the boat had been interviewed, and none of them knew anything."

My mouth turned down. "Dang. That's not helpful."

"Not really. There was a list of the people on the boat, though. I made a copy and put it in the glove box."

I opened the glove box and pulled out a folded paper. I unfolded it, and my eyes scanned it. "Eric Levitt, Amy Jackson, Greg Orwell, Neal Tanner, Ellie O'Hara, Jack McBride, Carrie Wilson, Cindy Baker, Tabitha Coats, Sandy Turner, Rita Kendell, Peter Olsen. I've met a few of them at the diner."

"Rita and Amy were both friends of Tabitha's. They didn't lose any money, so if it was one of them, that wasn't their motive. Ellie O'Hara got married a few years ago and moved. Jack McBride isn't around anymore. I think I heard he went to Topeka. Everyone else is still around."

"Do any of them seem more likely than the others?"

"Well, Carrie, Greg, Jack, and Peter all lost money because of Tabitha. She'd also dated Peter at one point."

"Interesting. Why did they break up?"

"I don't know. We didn't run in the same circles. Now that I think about it, she might have also dated Jack."

I grabbed a pen from my purse and scribbled a few notes next to the names. "So where was Stan Roberts when all of this happened? If he saw something, he must have been close."

"He was on one of the other boats. There's nothing in the case file about him, so if he saw something, he kept it to himself. It's really annoying to think he would withhold information on something this important. He always thought he was clever."

I drummed my fingers on the armrest of the truck. "Do you think he's really dead?"

He paused. "I did until you just said that. Do you think he isn't?"

"Well, it seems a little suspicious that a grave just popped up one day. Shouldn't there be a record somewhere if he died? I mean, he could have designed his own grave before he died, but who put it in the cemetery, and who would have buried him?"

Jett frowned as he turned into the library parking lot. "Once we get back, I'll make some calls. If we need to, we can get permission to dig up the grave and see if it's empty."

I shivered. "I'm not sure how eager I am for that."

"We'll only do it if we have to. If he died, there has to be a record of it somewhere. I need to figure out how the cemetery works. Someone has to be in charge of what goes on there. I would ask the mayor, but he's helpless."

"I didn't even know there was a mayor."

"He's nothing to brag about. He doesn't really do his job, and he keeps a low profile."

He parked, and we hurried into the library. A librarian was waiting for us and handed us two more books. Jett checked them out. Once we were back in the truck, we flipped through them.

"I don't see anything," Jett said.

"I guess I'll have to look harder at Barbra's."

"Something might be hidden in one. Maybe it wasn't as obvious as the first book." Jett turned on the truck and looked at me. "We could stop by the place that makes tombstones. I'd bet everyone comes here to get one. Are you up for it?"

"Yes, that's a good idea. They might have old records."

Jett backed out of the parking spot. "I'm still confused as to why Stan would do this. He loved a competition, but this seems to be going overboard."

"And it's not really a competition. He was putting a lot of confidence in luck. What if no one ever saw the clue?"

"Maybe he didn't care."

"When he died, what happened to his things? Did he have a house?"

"He did. Other people live there now."

"Did he have any family?"

"Not that I know of. A lot of things should have been done differently when the grave appeared. I don't think anyone gave any thought to whether it was legit. I wish the last sheriff was still around. Maybe he did look into it."

"Where is he?"

"He died." He grinned at me. "Nothing suspicious. I know how you think."

I shook my head. "I don't think everything is suspicious."

"Alright, I believe you."

"Liar."

He laughed as he pulled into another parking lot. "Here we are."

A small shop with tombstones out front stood before us. We entered the building, and I frowned. The dim lights made it hard to see anything after being outside. A tall man with glasses in a red polo shirt greeted us. "Hi, folks. Is there something I can help you with?"

Jett came forward. "Can I speak to the owner?"

"I'm the owner. Tyson Roberts."

"I'm Sheriff Jett Malone, and this is Ivy Clark. How long have you owned this place?"

"About twenty years."

"Do you make tombstones for towns around Wichita?"

He nodded. “Sometimes. I’m not the only one around, but I like to think we have the best quality and customer service.”

“Do you work with people from Muddy Creek?”

“I have.”

“Do you keep records?”

“Of course, Sheriff. Do you need me to look something up?”

“Yes, that would be great.”

“Come back to my office.” We followed him into a small room with a desk and computer. There were a few chairs against the wall.

Tyson went behind his desk and motioned to the chairs. “Pull up a chair and tell me what you need to know.”

We grabbed chairs and sat in front of the desk. Jett leaned forward. “Did you make a stone for a man named Stanley Bensen Roberts? This would have been about nine years ago.”

Tyson’s hands froze above his keyboard. He looked up at Jett, and his eyes narrowed. “I thought it had been long enough that no one would come.”

“Are you related?” I asked. “You have the same last name.”

He leaned back in his chair. “He was my cousin.”

“We didn’t know he had family.”

“Not a lot. Just me and my sister. I’m guessing you looked closely at his stone and realized it was nonsense?”

I nodded. There was no reason to bring up the book. "We were actually wondering if Stan is even dead."

He laughed, but his eyes were dull. "Oh, he's dead alright. I buried him myself."

Chapter 7

I leaned forward. "You buried him?"

Tyson took off his glasses and rubbed the bridge of his nose. "Yes. I own this place and the funeral home down the street."

Jett turned to me. "So he really is dead."

I frowned. "How did he die, and why can't I find his obituary?"

"He suffered from pancreatic cancer. When he became too weak to care for himself, he moved to a care facility in Wichita. He didn't want a funeral or an obituary. Just that stupid tombstone."

"Do you know what the tombstone meant?" I asked.

He shrugged. "I didn't want to. Stan's games always irritated me, and I wasn't happy about any of it. I knew it meant someday people would come by wondering what my crazy cousin was thinking. I'd hoped it had been long enough that it wouldn't matter."

"Do you know who owns the cemetery in Muddy Creek?"

"I do."

"I didn't know a person could own a cemetery," Jett said. "I thought it was the state or something."

"That's usually the way it is. Muddy Creek is too small to have its own. My grandfather started several in small towns, and they all belong to me now."

I leaned forward, my elbows on his desk. "It isn't well kept."

Tyson rolled his eyes. "I'm only one person. I can't afford to pay a bunch of workers to keep up all the places I own. I'm lucky if they get mowed twice a summer."

Jett sighed. "Can you tell us anything about Stan?"

Tyson rubbed his chin. "Stan was crazy. He thought he saw a girl get killed. He was sure he knew who did it—even though he was far away from where it happened and he wasn't wearing his glasses. Stan's eyesight was abysmal. I wouldn't trust him if he said he saw a cat five feet in front of him without his glasses."

"Did he tell you who he thought did it?" Jett asked.

"Of course not. With Stan, it was all about the game. He spent weeks in his room trying to figure out something clever. I would have called the police and told them he knew something if I thought he actually did. He didn't even decide he had seen it happen until he heard about her disappearance the next day."

"Was he on a boat when he thought he saw it?" I asked.

"Yes. It wasn't close, though. He said he could see two figures, but he couldn't make out who they were. Besides his lack of glasses, it was also dark, giving him no authority, in my opinion. He didn't actually see anything else. He just assumed it was the missing girl and guessed who he thought the other one was. I begged him to design a normal headstone, but he wouldn't."

"Why didn't he go to the police?"

Tyson crossed his arms. "That wasn't Stan's way. He's all about the game. If I were you, I would drop it. It's a waste of time and resources."

Jett looked at me. "It sounds like he was going on a guess."

"Perhaps," I said. "I'm not ready to give up."

Tyson shook his head. "Stan was always making people do foolish things. Don't let him make you look like a fool like he has so many others. His games aren't worth it."

We thanked him and left. I was tired and more confused than when we arrived. If Stan really was only going on a hunch, it would be hard to feel comfortable accusing someone, even if we solved his mystery. If it was dark, he didn't have glasses, and he hadn't seen someone get pushed, this was all a waste of time. Still, I needed to see what came of it all.

"What are you thinking?" Jett asked as he drove.

"So many things I can't make sense of them."

"I know what you mean."

I rested my head on the window and watched as small snowflakes fell. The next thing I knew, my head was jerking up, and we were in front of the diner. I quickly wiped at my mouth, hoping I hadn't drooled. There was the chance I'd snored, but I wouldn't ask.

Jett opened my door, and I grabbed the library books and jumped to the snow-covered ground. I checked my watch. The diner would still be open for another hour.

"Sorry I fell asleep."

He grinned. "It's alright."

"Why are you grinning like that? Did I do anything weird?"

His eyes twinkled. "Nope."

"Liar."

He shrugged. "There might have been light snoring."

"Ugh. I don't know why I'm so tired."

"I won't tell. It's probably from all the work you did at Barbra's. I have to go take care of a few things. I'll see you later."

"Bye." I went into the diner and glanced around. It was half full.

Boyd waved at me from a table with Barbra and Opal. "Hey, Ivy."

I didn't want to talk; I just wanted to sleep, but I had to make time for my best customers. "Hey! How are you guys doing?"

"Pretty good," Boyd said. "José's fried chicken really hits the spot."

Barbra nodded. "And the potatoes! Excellent."

Opal frowned. "He could mash them a bit more. There's nothing as disgusting as a lump in mashed potatoes."

Barbra rolled her eyes. "Ignore Opal. She's never satisfied."

Opal scowled.

Boyd scooted over and patted the bench. I reluctantly sat next to him. "Barbra was just telling us you're helping her with her house."

"Yep, and look at the poor thing," Barbra cooed. "You look exhausted, dear."

I smiled. "I'm a little tired, but I'm fine."

"Did you drop off all my loving belongings?"

I slapped myself on the forehead. "Oh no! We forgot!"

Barbra's eyebrow arched. "You didn't go to Wichita?"

"We did; we just forgot to go to the thrift store."

Barbra laughed. "So what did you and the sheriff do? You went all that way and forgot your purpose?"

Boyd chuckled. "I hope you two were sparking."

I rolled my eyes. "Don't be ridiculous. We went to two libraries and picked up some books. We also talked to... someone." I didn't need everyone to know what we were up to.

Barbra leaned forward, looking at the books on my lap. "Did you find the book?"

I placed the five books on the table. "We aren't sure. We checked out all the books they had, but it's hard to know if any of them is the right one."

Opal picked up a copy and frowned at the picture of the *Mona Lisa* on the cover. "You got five copies of the same book. And people think it's us old people getting senile."

I just smiled. I wasn't going to get into it all here. "Will you all excuse me? I need to take these upstairs."

"Of course," Barbra said.

I stood and hurried up to my room. I tossed the books on my bed and put my pajamas on. It was nice having José as the manager. I loved the diner, but it was nice not to have to be here all the time. I brushed my teeth and climbed into bed. Creepers jumped up next to me and curled up on my lap. I picked up one book and began going through it, page by page.

After finishing two books, I filled Creepers's food dish. He jumped to the floor and began eating. The next book didn't have anything. My eyes involuntarily closed. I would just rest them for a minute. The next thing I knew,

I was waking up. I looked at my clock. 2:30. I sighed and flipped on the lamp next to my bed.

Creepers was asleep on the foot of my bed, and I was freezing. I pulled up the covers and grabbed a book. It was much too cold. I wanted to turn up the heat, but that would require getting out of bed. I flipped open the book and began turning the pages. The pages were becoming a blur, and I almost missed it. Written in the margin near the spine with a blue pen, it said, "the biggest book in the library."

I smiled. I found it. A number 12 was also written next to it. Too bad the library wasn't open in the middle of the night. My teeth chattered. I dog-eared the page, something I rarely do, but I couldn't force myself to get out of bed. I pushed the book to the side and huddled deeper into my blanket. Everything on me hurt. I didn't have time to be sick. I had important things to do.

Chapter 8

Someone pounded on my door or my head; it was hard to know which. I pried my heavy eyelids open. Creepers stood by the door, looking up expectantly. There was another knock.

"Yes?" I croaked.

"Ivy? Are you alright?" José asked through the door.

I yawned and sat up. I glanced at my watch and hopped out of bed. It was after eleven. I put a hand to my head and waited for the spots to clear from my eyes.

"Ivy?"

I opened the door a crack and peeked out. José stood there in his white apron, wearing a big frown. "You look awful."

"Thanks. I feel awful." Creepers snuck past José.

"The contractor is here."

"Who?"

"The contractor who is going to expand the diner?"

My eyes widened. "Right. I can't go down like this."

"Have you changed any of your plans? I can talk to him."

"It's all the same. If you could talk to him, that would be great."

"Do you need a doctor?"

I coughed. "No, I just need to sleep."

"Call down if you need anything. Are you hungry?"

"No."

"Alright. I'll keep my phone close."

"Thanks." I closed the door and fell back into bed. I didn't have time to feel like this. Coughs wracked my body, and I grabbed a tissue from the nightstand. Once I caught my breath, I curled up on my bed and tried to go back to sleep. I looked at the messy pile of books and frowned. I needed to go to the library, but I couldn't go like this. Making Brian sick would be rude.

I grabbed my phone and scrolled down to Jett's number, then put the phone to my ear. It kept ringing, and I worried it would go to voicemail. When I was about to give up, he answered.

"Hello?" he said groggily.

"Hey, this is Ivy."

"What's up?" he mumbled.

"Are you alright?"

"Not really. I woke up with the plague or something."

"Me too. Well, I felt terrible before I went to bed."

He chuckled. "Did you call to compare symptoms?"

"No. I found something in one of the books last night. Since I don't feel like leaving my bed, I was going to have you go check at the library. I guess I'll just call Brian."

"What did you find?"

"In the margin, someone wrote 'Biggest book in the library.' Whatever it is, I hope it's still there."

"I would go, but I bet this is COVID or something. I can barely move, and a few people around have had it."

"Yeah, don't worry about it. I'll call Brian, then I'm hoping to pass out for a week."

"Alright. Take care."

"You too." I hung up the phone, then lay back down. I needed to rest before I could call someone else. There was another knock on the door.

"Yeah?"

"It's Boyd. José said you're feeling sick. Do you have any medicine?"

"No."

"What do you need, and I'll go get it?"

"I don't know. Jett thinks it's COVID. Maybe some Tylenol? I'm pretty sure I have a fever."

Boyd laughed. "So Jett's a doctor now?"

"He's sick too, and he said some people in town have had COVID."

"Alright. I'll be back in a few. Anything else you need?"

I glanced around my room, trying to spot my purse. "If I give you some money, do you think you could find me a blanket? I'm so cold."

"I'll grab you one. You can worry about paying me later. Anything else?"

"No."

I listened to him clomp down the stairs. I'd lucked out with the friends I'd made in Muddy Creek. Pulling my blanket up to my chin, I closed my eyes. I was supposed to be doing something, but I couldn't seem to remember what.

"I'm back!" Boyd said, pounding on the door. My eyes fluttered open, and I frowned. He was back? I thought I'd just closed my eyes. Boyd pushed open the door and walked in carrying two bags.

"Don't come in," I protested weakly. "You'll get sick."

"I'm old. Chances are, if it's out there, I've already had it." He set a bag on the floor and pulled a blanket from the other. He spread it over me and went for the other bag. Next, he grabbed a water bottle and a bottle of Tylenol. "If I don't come in, you might not take your medicine."

I wanted to protest, but he was probably right. Moving hurt. I forced myself to sit up, and Boyd handed me two capsules. I pushed them in my mouth and took the water he offered.

"Good girl. Now, do you need anything else?"

If I didn't feel so bad, I would have smiled. It was funny to see Boyd acting like a mother hen. "I found a clue." I pointed at the books. "It said to find the biggest book in the library."

Boyd grinned. "I'm on it." Turning, he disappeared through the door, but not before Creepers ran back inside. He jumped on the bed and rubbed his head against me. I checked that he still had food in his bowl, then I crawled back under the covers and closed my eyes. Creepers pressed his head into mine.

"Hey, buddy. I'm sorry I can't be fun right now." He jumped off the bed with a meow and ran to the windowsill. "Thanks for understanding." The truth was, I liked to play with Creepers way more than he liked to play with me. He would choose a scratching post over me every day of the week.

I didn't have time to be sick. Eleven people had been on the boat with Tabitha when she died. If I only talked to one each day, it would take over a week. It was anyone's guess how long I would be sick, and every day I missed was time lost. José and Boyd would help if I asked, but I didn't want to send them into potential trouble without me. Not that I could handle danger better than they could but I would feel guilty if anything happened to them.

The rest of the day was a blur. I was in and out of sleep. José brought me food a few times, and I tried to eat it. By dinner, my fever broke, and I woke up in a puddle of sweat. José came in with some soup and placed it by my bed.

"Thanks, José."

"You're welcome. I've been sending food over to Jett as well. He said he's already feeling better. How about you?"

"I do feel a lot better, though kind of gross. I bet I'll be fine by morning."

"It's always nice when these things come and go quickly." He paused as he was about to leave and opened his mouth as if to speak, but then shut it. "Well, have a good night."

"What were you going to say?"

He sighed. "I was just going to ask if you've heard from Boyd since this morning."

"Not since he came over. Why?"

"I'm sure it's nothing. He just said he would be over for lunch but never came. I tried to call him, and I sent him a text, but he never answered."

I sat up. "That's not like Boyd. He usually answers really fast."

"It's probably fine."

"Have you talked to Brian? Boyd was going to go to the library."

"No, maybe I'll call him."

I twisted my blanket in my hand. "What if he found a clue and tried to do something?"

José arched his eyebrow. "Like what?"

"I don't know. Maybe he's trying to find another one."

I caught José up on everything from yesterday. "I thought Boyd would find the biggest book at the library and bring it to me."

"I'll call Brian and then drive by Boyd's house before I go home. I'm sure there's no reason to worry."

I nodded. Shaking my head, I pushed the memory of him getting stuck in a tree last month from my head. It was probably safe to say he knew how to take care of himself or at least had his phone on him in case he needed help. I sighed. I wasn't going to sleep until I knew he was safe.

Chapter 9

I knew I was being ridiculous, but I couldn't help it. I pulled my boots over my socks and stuffed my arms into my purple coat. José had called me and told me Boyd hadn't gone to the library. That meant he'd left the diner, and something had happened between here and the library. Hopefully, he'd just remembered something he needed to do, but I wasn't chancing it. José was on his way to Boyd's house now. This was all making me nervous, and I wasn't going to solve anything from bed.

I pulled my hood over my head and went out into the frigid night air. My eyes scanned the street and walkways. I was looking for a bike track in the snow, but with all the footprints and tire tracks, I couldn't pick any out. Where would Boyd go?

I opened my car door and pulled out the snow scraper I had gotten the day before. There had been quite a variety, so I'd picked one with a long handle to make it easier. I brushed off the light sprinkling of snow and climbed in. How hard could driving in snow be? It wasn't deep. I started the car and cranked up the heat. I backed slowly from my spot and crept over the dark, empty road.

"No problem," I muttered. "It's just like driving with a slight crunch."

I talk to myself when I'm alone in the car. I'm not sure why. It helps me reassure myself when I'm not making the best decisions. I got to a stop sign and braked. The car didn't get the message. It slid into the middle of the intersection before it stopped. My heart thudded against my ribs, and I took a deep breath.

When I calmed myself enough to let off the brake, I began slipping again. I turned the wheel frantically and sighed with relief when I started going in the right direction. After a few close calls, I realized I did better if I didn't come to a complete stop. That was what made me slide. Thankfully, Muddy Creek only had five stop signs, and they could be avoided.

I turned onto a dark road just off the square and smiled when I saw bike tracks in the snow. They might not be Boyds, but I hadn't seen anyone else on a bike since it had been snowing. I drove slowly and followed the trail. It wasn't hard because there weren't any other tire tracks on this street.

A hill popped up in front of me, and I gulped. My fingers gripped the wheel, and I drove slowly to the top. I braked softly on my way down and prayed I would make it without slipping. The tires skidded a little, causing the car to beep at me. I looked down at a little light that let me know I was sliding.

"Thanks, I already know," I muttered to the car. "You don't have to make it worse by beeping at me." I got to the bottom, and the sliding stopped. I was going so slow I was hardly moving. This was the road to the cemetery. Why would Boyd go this way? We had a picture of the grave, so looking at it again wouldn't do any good.

It felt like an eternity, but I finally got to the cemetery. Boyd's bike was parked in the lot, but I couldn't see him. I pulled in and stopped the car. The cemetery didn't have any lights, so it was almost impossible to see anything. One thing I learned fast when I moved here was that it was scary dark at night. Without the light of the city, only the moon and stars give off light. The stars are amazing when there aren't any city lights.

I grabbed the snow scraper, stepped out of the car, and switched on my phone light. I shined it near Boyd's bike and spotted his footprints walking toward the cemetery. I took a breath of cold air and began following them. Boyd had better have a good explanation for coming out here.

Every horror movie I had ever seen was flashing through my head.

My brain was yelling at me to call someone. No one knew where I was, and that could be dangerous. I followed Boyd's prints up to Stan's grave. It looked like he had walked around it a few times and then moved off toward the trees.

"Come on, Boyd. You didn't go into the creepy trees, did you?" I dialed Jett's number, but it went straight to his voicemail. "Hey, Jett. This is Ivy. I'm at the cemetery… in the dark. Boyd's footprints go into the trees, so I'm following them. His bike is here. I just thought I would let you know in case I disappear or something. Ha ha. I'm sure it's fine. Bye."

I rolled my eyes. If that didn't sound pathetic, I didn't know what did. I should have thought it through first. Jett would probably wake up in the middle of the night, listen to my voicemail, and run over here. By the time he got it, I would probably be home.

I kept my snow scraper at my side and tried to walk casually after the footprints. If I didn't look panicked, I might convince myself I wasn't. Every noise made me jump. I was more worried about what animal might jump out at me than about finding a dangerous person. No one was crazy enough to be out here. Well, no one but Boyd. And me.

The footprints joined another set of footprints. The second set must belong to whoever I saw the last time we were here. It had snowed since then, so they must be new. I wondered if Boyd was following the prints or if he was with someone. I thought about calling out to him, but if someone else were out here, it would warn them. If there wasn't, I might just scare Boyd.

An owl hooted off in the distance, and I jumped, dropping my phone. I took a shaky breath and picked it up, shining it back on the tracks. Going slow wasn't getting me anywhere, so I picked up my pace. I wound around trees and walked down a gentle hill to a structure in front of me. I couldn't make it out well because of my small light, but Boyd's prints went toward it.

I walked forward, making as little sound as possible. The structure appeared to be a trailer like you would see in a trailer park. I frowned and shined my light in all directions. It was the only one I could see. I swallowed hard and kept my eyes on the prints. One set went up to the door, and one went past it to a window. The snow was packed down, so I guessed that Boyd had stood there for a while trying to see in. He'd eventually moved on.

I walked around to the side. Still no Boyd. It was freezing out here. It probably didn't help that I was still getting over being sick. I crept around to the back and saw prints going from the back door and into the woods behind. Boyd's tracks followed.

"Come on, Boyd," I muttered.

Something crunched behind me. I dropped my phone again and spun around, holding my snow scraper like a baseball bat.

José stood there holding up a lantern. He had a small grin on his face. "Sorry. I didn't mean to sneak up on you."

I lowered my weapon. "Dang it, José! I almost hit you! What are you doing out here?"

"You almost hit me? I'm almost ten feet away. I'm looking for Boyd, the same as you. I drove all over until I spotted his bike trail. When I saw your car and Boyd's bike in the parking lot, I chased you." He walked over to me. "Are you about to go deeper in? We should probably call Jett."

"I did. He didn't answer."

"Alright. Should we follow?"

I picked up my phone. "We have to. Come on."

José held up his lantern, and I felt safer somehow. I probably shouldn't have come alone. The lantern gave off a lot more light than my phone. I should probably keep a better light in my car.

I turned to José. "Do you know who lives in the trailer?"

He shook his head. "I'm not sure anyone does. Jack McBride owns this land, but he hasn't been around for years."

"Jack McBride? He was on the boat with Tabitha."

"We should probably talk a little quieter."

"Right." We walked for five minutes before we saw something on the ground ahead. "Boyd!" I took off toward the figure. Boyd lay in the snow, his hands and feet tied. He turned his head and smiled when he saw me. I dropped to my knees and began pulling at the bands.

"Took you long enough," he joked.

José reached us and pulled out a pocket knife. "Hold still, I don't want to cut you."

I sat back on my legs and waited for José to finish. "What are you doing out here? Why didn't you tell anyone where you were going?" I noticed the second set of footprints went even deeper into the trees, but I wasn't going to follow them.

Boyd's teeth chattered. "Can we talk about it later? Maybe once we get in a heated car?"

José finished untying him and helped him to his feet. "Can you walk?"

"Yep," Boyd said, rubbing his wrists. "I haven't been out here very long." We silently headed back toward the trailer. I kept looking over my shoulder to make sure no one was following us. I tried to think about what I'd heard about Jack McBride, but I couldn't come up with anything. All I knew was he was on my list of passengers on the boat. He might have been the one who moved to Topeka.

We passed the trailer and followed our footprints back up the small hill. I linked my arm with Boyd's and squeezed his arm. He smiled, but I could tell it was taking everything in him to keep walking. It felt like going back was a lot farther than coming in, but we eventually came out from under the tree cover. When the cars came into view, Boyd picked up speed. Headlights coming down the road made me nervous, but it was a public road. Anyone could drive here.

The lights turned on the cemetery road, and I let out a relieved breath when I recognized Jett's truck. He got to the parking lot and didn't take time to park. He jumped out of the truck, scanned the area, and ran toward us.

"What are you guys doing out here?" he called. We didn't answer. He was still too far away to have a conversation. When he reached us, he shined his flashlight on all of us. "Are you all okay? Boyd? You look chilled."

"He was tied up in the snow."

"Tied up?" He squinted into the dark trees. "Everyone in my truck."

"I drove," José and I said at the same time.

"I don't care, get in the truck. It's warm. You can come back for the cars tomorrow." We walked in silence to his truck and climbed in. I got in the back with José so Boyd could be closer to the heat.

Jett started the truck and flipped the heat to full blast. "I don't know what I'm going to do about you three. Why didn't you answer when I called you back, Ivy?"

I slid my phone out. "My phone must have been on silent."

He pulled out of the cemetery and clenched his jaw. "Don't ever go into danger. You should have gotten me when you realized Boyd might be in trouble."

"I did try to call you. I couldn't just hope you came around. Boyd would still be tied up if I hadn't gone."

"I would have found him," José said. "I was only a minute behind you. I hurried more when I saw your car and Boyd's bike in the lot."

Jett turned, and I'm sure he gave me a dirty look. It was hard to say in the dark. "Wait, you didn't even take José with you?"

"I didn't have time to round up a posse. I knew Boyd was out there somewhere."

"This is all my fault," Boyd said. "Can we wait and talk about it once I can control my chattering teeth?"

Jett shook his head but didn't say anything else. I wondered why we weren't talking about who might have tied Boyd up and perhaps calling in extra officers from another town. I'm not sure if it had registered to Jett yet that Boyd had been tied up. He was too distracted already when he'd come out here to find us. Jett was too young to have gray hair, but I was afraid I might be the one who caused them to come early.

Chapter 10

The four of us sat in a booth at the diner. We all had a mug of hot chocolate, and Boyd snuggled under a blanket. Jett wanted to take him to the hospital, but he refused to go. Boyd's color had returned to normal, and he relaxed against his seat.

"Alright, Boyd," Jett said. "What were you doing out in the woods all alone?"

Boyd took a sip from his mug. "Well, I was on my way to the library, and I thought I might check on the grave before it got too dark. I know we already looked at it, but I wanted to make sure we didn't miss anything. We didn't clean the snow from the sides last time, so I brushed off the snow, but I couldn't see anything."

"So you walked into the dark woods all alone?" I asked.

Jett raised his brow. "I'm not sure you're one to talk."

“I was going for a friend,” I protested.

Boyd shivered. “I saw someone looking at me, just like last time. I decided I might as well approach him and see what he was about. When I started toward him, he turned and disappeared into the trees. I followed his tracks to the trailer. I tried peeking in the window, but I couldn’t see anything. I’d gone that far, so I figured I’d get a good look around. When I went to the back, the door opened, and someone ran out.”

José grinned and shook his head. “So you followed again?”

“Course I did. I’m too old to wait these things out. After a minute, the man came toward me. He had some rope and a knife. He told me he could kill me or tie me up. I decided to go for the tying up.”

“Did you recognize him?” I asked.

“No. His face was covered with a big scarf.”

Jett rubbed the stubble on his chin. “Was it Jack McBride? That’s his land back there.”

Boyd pulled his blanket tighter. “Not unless he shrunk. Jack’s a tall man. This person wasn’t. At least, I don’t think he was. It was pretty dark by that point.”

I glanced at Jett. His eyes were a little puffy, and he blinked a lot. The illness we had wasn’t completely gone, and we were both feeling it. I wanted to put my head on the table and go to sleep.

“So he tied you up, and then Ivy and José found you?”

"Yep. You don't know how nice it is to have friends who look for you when you go missing. I worried it would be days before someone realized I wasn't just cooped up at home."

"So now what?" I asked.

Jett gave me a pointed look. "You stay out of this. I'm taking over. Before this, we didn't know whether anything was even happening. Now that we know something is really going on, I need to get serious about it."

"What if it isn't related?" José asked. "What if the man behind the cemetery has nothing to do with Tabitha? There's a good chance of it. What are the chances the person who killed Tabitha is just hiding in the trees and waiting for someone to come by and look at the graves? That doesn't make a lot of sense."

Jett nodded. "That's true. It's doubtful they would still be watching after ten years. Whoever it is was probably staying in Jack McBride's trailer. I didn't even know he had a trailer out there. I need to find out who and why. The three of you need to stay far away from the cemetery. Do you understand?"

I gave him my sweetest smile. "I understand that's what you want."

With a groan, he rested his elbows on the table and put his hands over his cheeks. "Come on, Ivy. Let me do my job. I can't have you out there looking for a possible murderer with nothing but your window scraper as a weapon."

I nodded. "I really should get a better weapon."

"Look, you let me deal with the trailer and whoever is out there, alright? You can go to the library and try to figure out the clues. Is it a deal?"

I pushed a piece of hair behind my ear and frowned. "For now."

José laughed, and Jett sighed. "What do you mean for now?"

I shrugged. "I'll follow the clues from the books, but what if they lead me to the cemetery or to the trailer?"

He rubbed his eyes. "Then you come tell me. Okay?"

I nodded. "Alright. Any word on getting a deputy? You seemed to think you might get one."

He leaned back. "There is a cop from Illinois who's interested in coming down here. He's still getting approval, but he could be here in a month or so."

"That will be nice. Then you won't have to do everything on your own."

"True. I'm looking forward to it."

Muddy Creek is small, and it's hard to get anyone to come work here. Jett came to be sheriff after a few years as a police officer in California. He didn't like the big city, so he came at the urging of his parents. No one else was running for sheriff, so he got the job by default. He'd been here a while with only the occasional help from the police in Wichita.

"Sorry I got all you sick people out of bed," Boyd said. "I'm feeling just fine now so if someone will drop me off at home I'll leave you all alone."

"I'll take you and José home," Jett said. "No one else has a car until we go pick them up tomorrow. Ivy, you go straight to bed."

I gave him a half smile. "Alright, Dad. And are you going to go to bed as well?"

"After I go check out the woods. If someone dangerous is out there, I need to find them."

My smile slipped. "Call for backup. You can't go in alone."

He sighed. "I was planning on it."

I nodded. I watched them leave, then locked the door behind them. When I got upstairs, I found Creepers splayed across my entire pillow, and he didn't look like he was going anywhere. I pulled off my coat and boots and sighed. I still felt weak and tired, so I fell into bed without changing. My head was at the foot of the bed so I wouldn't disturb Creepers. I'd learned quickly that a tired cat isn't a happy cat.

I closed my heavy eyes, but I knew sleep wasn't coming. Who would be out in the woods? If the trailer belonged to Jack McBride, but the person who tied Boyd up wasn't Jack, then who was it, and why were they out there? Boyd saw them come out of the trailer, so they were borrowing it or trespassing.

It bugged me that someone had watched us when we were at the cemetery, and someone had watched Boyd tonight. What were the chances someone was out hiding in the trees only on the days someone was at Stan Robert's grave? Not high, in my opinion. If it was the person who killed Tabitha and they were staying in the woods, then had they been watching the cemetery for ten years. That also seemed unlikely.

Creepers woke up and left my pillow to lie on my stomach. I was getting on my pillow if he was going to do that. I picked him up and repositioned myself. Creepers settled against me, and I rubbed his back. With luck, I would feel better tomorrow, and I could start searching the library.

Chapter 11

The following morning, I felt great. Especially considering the small amount of sleep I'd gotten the night before. I made two pans of brownies and experimented with their overall appearance. I stood at the enormous kitchen island and looked at my work. First, I tried making a flower on the tops with a stencil and powdered sugar. It was alright, but it smeared every time. I tried small decorations made from piping frosting, and that was going a little bit better than the powdered sugar.

"I like it," José said, looking over my shoulder.

"It could be better."

"Hold your arm at an angle. Here, watch." José picked up one of my bags of frosting and made a perfect leaf on top.

"Nice."

"If you do it enough, it becomes natural."

"Have you called Boyd today?" I asked. "I keep wondering about him."

"He called me first thing in the morning to let me know he doesn't want to be left out of anything."

"That sounds like Boyd."

"I thought you would be at the library this morning."

"I want to be, but I want to make sure I'm keeping up with the desserts here."

"We have enough help now that you probably only need to bake what you want to."

I nodded. "How is the sign-up for Thanksgiving going?"

He grinned. "Way better than I thought it would. We'll have a full house."

"Nice." I was happy I didn't have to spend Thanksgiving alone. "How many pies do you think we'll need?"

"I don't know. We should have asked people what their favorites are."

"Should we have a variety for people to choose from, or just a few but make a lot?"

"Hmm. It's hard to say. We have to have pumpkin and apple pie at least. Those seem to be the big ones if we go by what people have been ordering this month." We had been serving pie all month, but we only had two choices a day.

I wrinkled my nose. "I love pumpkin muffins, but I hate pumpkin pie. Apple isn't my favorite either."

José smirked. "Don't tell me you're a pecan pie lover?"

I shrugged. "It's alright."

"So what is your favorite?"

"I don't want to tell you because you'll tease me."

José arched his eyebrow. "Please tell me it isn't pudding pie."

I grinned. "Chocolate cream pie. I'll eat banana as well."

José put a hand to his heart and groaned. "Cream pies aren't really pie!"

I laughed. "I just don't like the texture of most pies. The warm fruit with the crust just feels wrong. I can eat it to be polite, but I don't want to."

"Cream pies are for little kids."

I just smiled and tried making another flower on a brownie.

"Okay, I vote we do pumpkin, apple, pecan, cherry, and chocolate cream. How does that sound?"

I grinned. "Sounds good to me."

"I also vote you make the chocolate pies. Stirring the pudding takes so long. Using instant doesn't taste as good."

"That's fine."

"José, your burger is burning," Anton said.

"Shoot." José hurried over to the large skillet.

Carrie came over to me and gestured to the brownies. "Do you want me to help? Things are a bit slow today, and I'm pretty good at piping flowers."

"Sure, thanks." This was great. I'd wanted to speak with Carrie, but I hadn't figured out a way to do it without seeming weird. I still wasn't sure how to approach it.

Carrie grabbed a bag and began making flowers. They were better than mine. "The other day, you brought up Tabitha."

My head shot up, and I looked at her. Her eyes stayed on her work.

"Were you really looking for a cat name, or were you talking about Tabitha Coats?"

I rubbed my lips together as I thought. "I was talking about Tabitha Coats."

"I thought so. I saw the way José tried to get you to be quiet. People are talking about the last two mysteries you solved. I figured you must be looking into it or something."

"I noticed you were on the same boat as Tabitha."

"Yeah, I was. I wasn't happy about it either."

"Oh?"

"I hated Tabitha with a fiery passion. That's no secret, and I'm not the only one."

"Because you lost money when you invested in her company?"

She still hadn't looked up. She kept piping frosting. "No. Yes. Well, It's complicated. I hated her before I lost money. I just hated her more after."

"Why did you hate her before?"

She sighed and glanced up at me. "I dated Jack McBride about a hundred years ago. He's before your time here, but I'm guessing you know about him?"

"I know he was on the boat."

"Yes, that entire vacation was a nightmare. Jack and I dated after high school and for a few years after. Jack was a manipulator, and I finally realized it. Before I could break up with him, Tabitha got involved. Have you seen any pictures of her?"

"No."

"Well, she was drop-dead gorgeous and as much of a manipulator as Jack. I saw them walking around town holding hands. I was done with Jack, but it still made my blood boil. Couldn't he man up and tell me we were over? I hated both of them from that point on."

"So Tabitha dated Jack and Peter?"

Carrie waved her hand in dismissal. "She dated everyone. Peter only lasted a month."

"How long did she date Jack?"

"About a year. They were a horrible pair. They were always fighting."

"So they weren't dating when she died?"

"No."

"It seems strange you were all on the same boat. Wasn't that awkward?"

Her brows went up. "I can't even tell you how much. When I got to the retreat and saw that I was on a boat with Tabitha and Jack, I was really upset. My sister had just gotten married and hadn't come. We could request one roommate, but I hadn't requested any. I tried to get it changed, but no one wanted to be with Tabitha except her two friends. The boat was full of people who hated her."

"Interesting. I'm surprised she stayed around after making so many enemies."

"She had no problems with people disliking her. She acted like it was our problem."

I nodded. "Do you think her death was an accident?"

"I don't know. All I know is, everyone on that boat hated her, except her friends. Any of us could be seen to have a motive. I didn't do it, but I didn't feel bad about it either."

The brownies all had little flowers on top. Carrie was fast. "Thanks for helping me. And for telling me about Tabitha."

"Sure. I figured I should tell you what I know since being quiet only makes people look guilty."

I had one more question but didn't know how to ask delicately. "I'm sorry to ask this, but is there a reason you invested with Tabitha when you hated her? Same with

Peter and Jack. If they dated her, why would they invest with her?"

Carrie sighed. "I can't say why Peter and Jack did it. For me, it just seemed like a good way to get money fast. Tabitha always seemed so confident, so I felt sure I would make money. I cringe thinking back now."

"Thanks for telling me."

"Have you talked to Rita Kendall or Amy Jackson? They were both Tabitha's friends. They might have unique insights about who might have done it."

"I haven't. That's a good idea, thanks." It really was a good idea. Friends were more likely to point a finger and know what Tabitha thought about everyone else. That could wait, though. First, I was going to run by the library. I needed to find the biggest book Brian had.

Chapter 12

"Hey, Ivy." Brian greeted me when I entered the library. "You have that look in your eyes. Did you figure something out?"

I smiled. "We checked out a few copies of *The Da Vinci Code* from the Wichita library."

"Any luck?"

"Yes. One of them had a note in the margin."

"What did it say?"

"The biggest book in the library."

Brian grinned. "*War and Peace*. No contest. Come on, let's find it."

"Don't you need to see if it's checked out?"

He chuckled. "No one ever checks that monster out." I followed him around a corner and down an aisle. His eyes ran over a shelf, and he pulled out a gigantic brown book and handed it to me.

"That is big." I opened it to reveal yellowed pages. The cover was in good shape, and it looked like it hadn't been read much, considering how old it must have been.

"The only time I remember it being checked out was when one of the high school boys was trying to impress someone. I asked him if he liked it, and from what he said, I'm guessing he didn't get past the first ten pages."

"Have you read it?"

Brian crossed his arms and winked. "You know I have. I have my own copy."

"Stan was really pushing his luck when he planned this out. It seems like some of these books could have disappeared before they were needed."

"That is probably part of the fun for him. He had to know there was a huge chance no one would figure it out or even try."

I flipped through the book and saw nothing obvious. "I'll check this out." We walked back to the front desk. "Do you know where Amy Jackson or Rita Kendall live?"

"Yep. I can show you on my map," he said, pulling it from his desk. He opened it up and circled two houses. They were on opposite sides of town. "I guess you're getting to the interviewing part of your investigation?"

"Yes, I keep putting it off."

"Well, good luck." He handed me the book, and I tucked it under my arm.

"Thanks."

As I left the library, I almost ran into Boyd.

"Ivy! Are you working on the case without me?"

I handed him the book. "I just came to get the book."

"*War and Peace*. Outstanding book."

"You've read it?"

He laughed. "No, and I don't ever plan to."

"Well, that's the biggest book Brian has."

"Have you looked through it?"

"Not well. I'm going to drop it off with José, then go talk to Amy Jackson."

"I'm coming."

"You should be home resting."

"What about you? You were sick yesterday."

"I'm feeling fine today."

Boyd nodded. "Me too."

"Okay, let's go."

We walked to the diner, and I wondered how I would survive once it got below freezing. This was cold enough for me, but from what everyone said, I was in for a colder winter. When we got in sight of the diner, we saw Jett walking toward us. I waved, and he waved back.

"Hello," I said when he met up with us.

"Hi. I was looking for you two."

"Oh, yeah?"

"I found this note on the sheriff's office door last night after I dropped everyone off at home." He handed me a sticky note.

I squinted down at it. "Boyd Webster is tied up in the woods on the north side of the cemetery."

Boyd peeked at the note. "That means whoever tied me up didn't want to leave me for dead. It also means they know me. I sure didn't introduce myself last night."

I tapped my lip. "That means whoever did it probably isn't a killer."

"Not necessarily," Jett said. "Just because they didn't want to kill Boyd doesn't mean they didn't kill Tabitha."

Boyd grinned. "I am a lot more likable than she was. I feel better knowing someone didn't leave me out there to die."

Jett took the note back. "If they know you, you must know them. Is there anything you can remember that might help?"

"Nope. It was dark, and he didn't say much. His voice didn't seem familiar, but he was obviously trying to sound deeper than his normal voice."

"I took the note in to have it scanned for prints. There weren't any."

"Brian found the next book," I said, holding it up. "We should have him help us more. We would still be trying to figure out the *Da Vinci Code* without him."

Jett grinned, but it looked forced. "And it doesn't hurt that he's got the whole tall, dark, and handsome thing going on."

"Who? Brian?" I asked. Brian was good-looking, but so was Jett. Was he trying to imply that was the reason I wanted Brian to help?

Boyd laughed softly.

Jett cocked his head. "I'm just joking. Did you find a clue?"

"Not yet."

"I wonder if this would all be easier if we looked through all the library books and tried to find all the clues at once."

"I think it would be easy to miss something," I said. "We can do that, but I think it should be a last-ditch effort. Even when I had the last book, it took time to find it."

Jett nodded. "I need to go check on something at my office. Let me know if you find anything."

I nodded. "We will." I rushed into the diner and gave the book to José. Within a few minutes, we were walking to Amy Jackson's house. I would've preferred driving, but my car was still at the cemetery, and it wasn't a quick walk.

We stopped in front of a red brick rambler and walked up to the door. I rang the bell, and a dog barked inside. The door opened, and a woman about thirty-five poked her head out. I recognized her from town. She was wearing yoga pants, and her brown hair was pulled into a ponytail.

"Hello," she said. "Do you want to come in? I've been expecting you."

I looked at Boyd, and he shrugged. "Sure." She moved back and let us enter. A small black-and-brown Yorkie barked at us while wagging his tail.

"Knock it off, Barney," she said to the dog. "Sorry, he loves barking at everyone. He's harmless."

She led us to a sitting room and had us sit on a brown leather sofa. She sat across from us on a matching loveseat.

"Why were you expecting us?" I asked.

"It's a small town. Everyone is talking about you, and how you are trying to find Tabitha's murderer. I figured it was only a matter of time before you came asking questions. I'm glad you came now because I've been keeping my house clean in case you came. That isn't easy with this little terror." She picked up the dog, and he rested on her lap.

"Thanks for talking to us," I said.

"Sure thing. You've done wonders with Sue's Diner. I'm sure your grandma would be proud."

"Thanks. It's been fun."

"So I guess you want to know where I was when Tabitha was pushed?"

"You think she was pushed?" I asked.

"Doesn't everyone?"

"I thought most people believed it was an accident."

She crossed her legs and leaned back. "That's unlikely."

"Why?"

"Tabitha was many things, but brave wasn't one of them. She was scared of the water. I was shocked when she went on the boat. She didn't know how to swim. She's also scared of being out in the dark. I seriously doubt she would have gone out on the deck by herself."

"Do you have any suspicions about who could have done it?"

"Not anything concrete. Everyone hated Tabitha."

Boyd leaned forward. "Everyone except you and Rita?"

She laughed. "Oh, Rita and I hated her too. We were just scared of her."

My eyes narrowed. "What do you mean?"

"Tabitha was the most popular girl in school because everyone feared her. She decided Rita and I would be her friends, and we were too scared to do anything about it. Being on her bad side wasn't a good place to be so we dealt with her. She bossed us around and made us miserable, but we didn't want to cross her."

"If you had to guess who did it, who would you think did it?" I asked.

Amy shrugged. "It's hard to say. She did a lot of low-down garbage to everyone on the boat. I wouldn't be shocked if any of them did it."

"Did you do it?" Boyd asked.

She tilted her head and frowned. "No, Boyd. You know me better than that. My life was instantly better without her around, but I didn't do it."

"Are you still friends with Rita?" I asked.

"No. We weren't really friends to begin with. We didn't do anything together after it happened. If we run into each other, we talk for a minute, but that's it."

"We know she dated Jack and Peter. Do you know why she broke up with them?"

"Let's see. It's been so long. She only dated Peter for a short time because she was trying to make Jack jealous. She'd had her eye on Jack for some time, but he was dating Carrie Wilson. That made Peter really mad. I'm not sure what happened between her and Jack. She wouldn't talk about it, and it made her angry, so I wonder if he broke up with her."

"So she dated two people who were on the boat." I already knew this, but it was good to have confirmation.

"Two?" She laughed. "She dated every guy on the boat at least once."

I pulled out the list. "Greg, Neal, Jack, Peter, and Eric?"

"Yep. She only dated people long enough to get something from them. She used anyone she could."

I tapped my fingers against my leg. "Why would someone put all her enemies together on the boat? That sounds a little odd."

"Those weren't all her enemies. She had plenty on the other boats. She went too far with her little scheme. That burned the last of her bridges around here. I think she even knew it. She was planning on moving out of Muddy Creek, and I think it's because she realized no one would ever trust her again."

A new thought was forming in my mind. What if someone set the whole thing up? What if they placed people they knew disliked Tabitha on the boat and just hoped something would happen?

Chapter 13

The pie crust looked like garbage. Something was wrong with it. Crusts were supposed to be crumbly, but this was ridiculous. It wouldn't stay together. I'd never made good pies. I wonder if it was because I didn't really care for them.

"It happened again," I said to José. "I can't make it so that it doesn't fall apart."

José raised his brow from his spot at the island. He was rolling out a perfect crust. "I told you I can do these. You work on the graham cracker crusts."

"Alright," I said, admitting defeat. I scraped the crust from the island and tossed it. The diner was closed, but we were still preparing for Thanksgiving tomorrow. I was more excited than I should be. Turkey and mashed potatoes were my favorite. I would eat it more, but cooking a turkey for one person seemed pointless.

I grabbed a bag of graham crackers and a freezer bag. The back door opened, and Jett came in.

"It smells like apple pie," he said, taking off his tan jacket and tossing it on a stool. "I can't wait until tomorrow. I hope you make enough pie."

I glanced up at him. "Wait, are you coming tomorrow?"

"Yep. My parents made a reservation. Mom hates to cook. She was thrilled when she found out the diner was offering Thanksgiving dinner."

I opened a bag of crackers and dumped them in the freezer bag. "I don't think I've met your parents."

"They don't come to town much."

I took a rolling pin and used it to crush the crackers. "Are you here for a reason, or just to make sure we make enough pie?"

He laughed. "I just saw the light on and thought I'd drop in. You really should lock the door after hours."

My eyes sparkled. "That's true. You never know who might wander in."

He grinned, and I had the most ridiculous urge to walk up and kiss the stubble on his jaw. I felt my face turn tomato red, and I returned to the cracker crushing. I really was ridiculous. It would be nice to have a friend my age to talk to about things like this. I loved José and Boyd, but they are not the people I want to share my deepest feelings with. I'm sure they would love to tease me about it.

"When are the renovations starting?" Jett asked, snitching a piece of apple.

"With luck, next week. But if it snows, they might have to put it off."

"Will you have to close the diner?"

"I hope not. Most of the stuff will happen out back and on top, so I'm not too worried."

"That's good."

"Hey, I know Boyd will be annoyed he isn't here, but I have a thought I wanted to run by you guys."

José smirked. "Oh, I thought you forgot I was here."

I tilted my head and glared at him. "I knew you were here."

His eyes danced. "What did you want to tell us?"

I leaned against the island, facing Jett and José. "Everyone on the houseboat hated Tabitha. I also found out she dated every guy who was on it."

Jett frowned. "Are you sure?"

"That's what Amy said."

"Well, I guess she would know."

"Amy and Rita didn't even like her. They were scared of her. What if someone purposely put them all together on the boat, hoping that someone would kill her?"

Jett's eyes narrowed. "Hmm. That sounds a little far-fetched. If someone did that, they expected something very unlikely to happen."

José put his crust in a pie tin. "Maybe whoever made the boat assignments just put them all together as a punishment for Tabitha and just didn't realize how bad it would be."

I sighed. "I guess so. Can we find out who made the assignments, though?"

"Perhaps," Jett said. "I mean, someone was obviously in charge. I'm not sure who to ask."

"The mayor would have been the one to ask," José said. "He was the one making most of the calls."

"Who was the mayor back then?"

"Mayor Bowin. He died about a year ago."

I frowned. That figured. "Did you have time to look through the library book?" I asked José.

"Not really. I flipped through it, but the diner was busy… and then I forgot. Sorry."

"It's alright. How many more pies do we need to make? I can look through it afterward."

"We probably need one or two more fruit pies and a few more chocolate."

"I should have had us start earlier."

José shrugged. "It will be fine. Maybe two more hours."

"Is your staff working tomorrow?" Jett asked. "Are you going to be short-handed?"

"We aren't having anyone work," José said. "I can handle the food, and we're going to do it buffet style so people can get what they want and go back for more."

"Nice. I'm excited. It's been a long time since I've had real Thanksgiving food. Last year, my mom made tacos, and the year before, we had frozen pizza. I don't think my mom knows how to bake a turkey."

I smiled. "Well, it's a good thing we decided to leave the diner open."

"Yeah. I'm happy about it. How many people are coming?"

"About forty."

"That's a good amount. I'll have to come early to get a good table."

I grabbed a stick of butter from the fridge, put it in a bowl, and put it in the microwave. "Did you ever go look in the woods around the cemetery?"

Jett nodded. "I had a few officers from Wichita come in and help me. Since the snow didn't last, there weren't any footprints. We didn't find signs of anyone. I want to go look in Jack McBride's trailer, but I can't find any sign of him."

"Does he have any family around?"

"No. His parents both passed away a few years ago. He was an only child. He's got to be somewhere, but no one I've talked to knows where. The taxes on his land get paid every year. He hasn't sold his land."

"Did he live in the trailer when he lived here?"

"No. His family had a house in town. I don't know if anyone lived in the trailer. Do you, José?"

"No. I've never known of anyone living there. I didn't even know the trailer was out there."

"What is Jack like?" I asked.

Jett picked up another apple slice. "Conceited is the first thing that comes to my mind."

José nodded. "It wasn't surprising when he dated Tabitha. They were similar in a lot of ways. Neither of them thought twice about inconveniencing anyone."

"Did he have friends? It seems weird he would grow up in such a small town, and no one would know where he went."

Jett sat on a stool. "He had friends. I've talked to everyone I know of, but he hasn't contacted any of them since he left."

I moved my jaw from side to side. "That sounds suspicious to me. Who leaves the only home they know and never contacts anyone again? It sounds like he's trying to stay away."

"Could be."

José pulled a pie from the oven. "What I want to know is why no one heard anything from Tabitha when she fell into the lake. If I fell or got pushed, I think I would automatically scream."

I took the melted butter from the microwave and set it on the island to cool. "If I was about to fall into a lake, I would probably hold my breath, not scream."

"No one heard a splash?"

"It was pretty late. Everyone was probably asleep."

"How many people have you talked to?" Jett asked. "I think you should leave it to me."

"I've only talked to Amy and Carrie."

"I've talked to most of them."

I crossed my arms. "When?"

"I've talked to a few of them each day for about three days."

"And you didn't tell me?"

He grinned. "I didn't realize you were my supervisor."

I tilted my head and tried to give him a stern look but I'm pretty sure my eyes gave me away. "Did anyone say anything interesting?"

"Not really. They all claim they were asleep. Rita might be avoiding me."

"I don't know her. She's the other one who was supposedly Tabitha's friend."

"Yeah. I knocked on her door two days in a row, and she didn't answer. I'm pretty sure I saw the curtains move the first day."

José stuck another pie in the oven. "Anyone avoiding the sheriff must be hiding something."

Jett nodded. “That’s what I’ve been thinking, although Rita has always been on the quiet side.”

“Aren’t all these people around your age?” I asked.

“Most of them are a few years older. Tabitha would have been thirty-five if she was still alive. I think Jack was a couple of years older than the rest.”

“I feel like we aren’t going to get anywhere until we either find Jack or solve the clues in the books.”

“You might be right. The day after tomorrow, I’ll work harder to find Jack. Working on Thanksgiving won’t be helpful because anyone with any resources will be out of the office.”

Chapter 14

The entire diner smelled divine. José should be proud. All the food was loaded onto the kitchen island. We'd covered it with an enormous gold tablecloth. We rarely let people into the kitchen, but we couldn't figure out a better place to do a buffet.

Decorating the booths had been fun. We put gold cloths on all the tables and cute pumpkin centerpieces in the middle. I'd found some turkey salt and pepper shakers online and had a set on each table. José had even gotten butter in the shape of a turkey. They would be adorable until the first person cut into them.

The dining area was already close to being filled. We promised to start at exactly five o'clock, and I was sticking to that. I peeked out the window from the kitchen to the dining area and gazed around at the happily chatting people. Boyd was at a table with Barbra, Opal, and another woman. Jett sat with an older man and woman who must be his parents. Almost every table was filled.

I went back into the kitchen and looked at the clock. Only two more minutes. José was putting the final touches on the turkey. I grabbed my cat apron and pulled it over my head. I wanted Jett's mom to know I appreciated the effort she put into making it. I still couldn't believe he'd done that for me.

"Ready?" I asked José.

"Yep. This is going to be perfect. Do you want to go tell everyone they can start, or should I?"

"Why don't you do it? You did most of the cooking."

José beamed. "Okay, thanks." He left the kitchen, and I took a deep breath. There was nothing to be nervous about. José had it all under control.

People started filing into the kitchen, their plates in hand. It would have been nicer to serve people, but then they couldn't get what they wanted, and we would have had to make people work on the holiday. This way, people could eat as much as they wanted, and we wouldn't end up with too many leftovers.

I greeted people as they came in. It was too bad the old jukebox didn't work. Not that I knew any Thanksgiving songs to play, but a little music might be nice. The diner had a sound system, but it was getting old. I should probably talk to the contractors about it the next time they come.

Jett entered the kitchen with his parents. His dad was as tall as he was, and his mom was at least two inches taller than my five foot five. Jett's dad had gray hair and wore a plaid shirt that reminded me of Boyd. His mother had brown curly hair and wore a long blue dress. Someone stopped Jett, and his parents moved to the island without him.

I moved closer to the couple and smiled. "You must be the Malones. I'm Ivy Clark."

Mrs. Malone's eyes sparkled as she shook my hand. "We've been meaning to come introduce ourselves, but there is always so much to do on the farm. I'm Carol, and this is Tanner."

Mr. Malone shook my hand. His hand was calloused, and he had a firm grip. "Jett talks about you all the time. It's nice to finally meet you."

Carol winked. "And bless you for wearing that hideous apron."

My eyes went wide. "You did a wonderful job with it."

She laughed. "My sewing is superb, but that material? Aye, I almost passed out when Jett told me he wanted me to sew it into an apron for you. He was so excited I didn't have the heart to tell him how ugly it was going to be."

A small giggle slipped from my lips. "It was nice of him to have it made for me. He knows I love cats."

"It would have been nice if he'd avoided neon colors. Still, it was kind of you to pretend you liked it, and it's brave of you to wear it. I'm sure no one would blame you if it fell into the disposal or something equally destructive."

"Cherry pie," Tanner said, pointing at the desserts. "Cherries stain like crazy. Just drop a piece right on the apron."

I laughed. "It's already fading. I'm messy, so I have to wash it often."

Carol raised her brow. "How often do you wear it?"

"About twice a week."

"Interesting. I wouldn't wear something like that more than once unless I really cared about the person who gave it to me."

Fire crept up my neck and into my face.

Tanner shook his head. "I only saw you wear the cow earrings I gave you once."

She patted him on the arm. "We've been together long enough I know it's not going to hurt your feelings."

He arched his brow. "Are you sure about that?" He laughed. "That's why I let you pick out all your presents now. I've learned a surprise is only appreciated if it's a good one. I have horrible taste that I've apparently handed down to my son."

I smiled and hoped my face wasn't the same color as the cherry pie. "I'll let the two of you get some food. It was really nice meeting you."

"You too, hon," Carol said. "We can see why Jett talks about you so much."

I forced another smile and moved away from the crowd. I pulled my water bottle from the fridge and took a long drink. Did wearing the apron make everyone in Muddy Creek think I had a thing for Jett? I hoped I wasn't that transparent.

"Ivy," Jett said from behind me.

I spun around and grinned. "Hey, Jett."

He looked over his shoulder to where his parents were loading their plates with food, then turned back to me. "I hope my parents didn't say anything weird."

"No, they were great. Nice people."

He tilted his head. "You bolted away from them pretty fast, and you looked a little... red."

Why did my face turn red so easily? "I just needed some water."

"Are you sure that was all?"

I laughed. "What do you want it to be?"

"Nothing, I just know my parents and they can say some awkward things. Especially my mom. I hope they didn't embarrass you."

"No, not at all," I lied. "You should go get some food. You don't want to let it get cold."

"Why don't you come sit with us?"

"I need to make sure all the dishes stay filled. It wouldn't be Thanksgiving if we ran out of potatoes or something."

"I've got it, Ivy," José said, approaching us. "Go eat with the Malones."

"I can't leave you in here alone."

"I'm by an island full of food. People will come and go all night. Go."

"Thanks," I said, wondering how José could be so dense he couldn't tell I would be uncomfortable with Jett and his parents. How would I enjoy my food when I had to worry about impressing the Malones? I knew it shouldn't matter, but I wanted them to like me.

My cat apron was already dirty, so I tossed it in a bin. I was glad I'd taken the time to curl my hair and put on a cute red sweater. I grabbed a plate and followed Jett to the line. All the guests seemed to be enjoying themselves as they piled food onto their plates and talked to their friends and family. I was glad we'd opened. If we hadn't, I would probably be eating a frozen burrito like José had said.

Thanksgiving food was my favorite. I usually mixed it all together, but my mom made me promise I would never do that in public. I could wait and do that tomorrow with any leftovers. It was amazing how much food Jett could load onto one plate. I would be impressed if he could get back to the table without spilling.

Once we got our food, we went out and sat across from his parents.

"Ivy is going to join us," Jett said.

Carol grinned and reached over to pat my hand. "Lovely."

Tanner was busy shoving half a roll into his mouth. His plate looked just like Jett's.

"So you are from Arizona?" Carol asked. "Do you miss it?"

"Not as much as I thought I would. Muddy Creek is so small, but I really like it here."

"Well, we are glad you're here. I've only heard good things about you. It's too bad you aren't qualified to be Jett's deputy. You're making a name for yourself out here. Imagine solving two murders. It's impressive."

"I would be a horrible deputy," I said. "Just ask Jett. I might have helped with those other cases, but I'm not very good at following the rules."

"That's for sure," Jett said right before he took a bite of potatoes.

Carol laughed. "It's good for Jett. He needs someone to challenge him now and then. Being an only child made him a little soft."

Jett rolled his eyes. "I'm not soft."

Carol smiled at him. "It's only to be expected. I was almost forty when he was born, and I'd given up on ever having children. He was a miracle, and we might have spoiled him a little."

Jett turned to me. "They have a funny definition of spoiled. I started helping on the farm when I was so young

I don't remember it. I worked every day after school until I went to college."

"Jett is a hard worker," Tanner said, "but he got most everything he wanted."

"Why are we having this conversation?" he asked.

"You must be proud of him," I said. "He's a great sheriff."

Tanner puffed out his chest. "The best Muddy Creek has ever had."

Carol nodded. "That's for sure. We were so happy when he agreed to come here. It's not easy being the only law around here."

"Did I tell you Ivy is expanding the diner?" Jett asked, changing the subject.

"Yes, that's exciting," Carol said. "Do you know how long it will take?"

"A few months, depending on the weather. I probably shouldn't have done it in the winter, but the contractor offered me a deal to do it now. I guess they have difficulty finding work during this time of year."

"I would imagine."

The bell above the door jingled, and I glanced over. A woman in her thirties walked in. She pushed her reddish-brown hair from her eyes and glanced around. She looked familiar, but I couldn't place her.

Jett leaned toward me. "That's Rita Kendell."

I nodded. She was the other woman who had been friends with Tabitha. The one who had been avoiding Jett. She hadn't been on the reservation list, but we had plenty.

When her gaze landed on our table, her mouth turned down. Her eyes locked on mine. "I'm not talking to the sheriff," she said loud enough that the entire room turned to look at her. She pointed at me. "I will talk to you. I know who killed Tabitha Coats."

Chapter 15

Rita turned and left the diner. The silence that had fallen over the room after Rita's declaration was broken as everyone began talking at once.

I turned to Jett, and we shared a look.

"Go," he said. "I'll watch from the window."

I jumped up from my seat and followed Rita. She stood on the sidewalk outside the diner in the light snow, pulling her coat tight around herself. The bitter air nipped at my face, and I regretted not grabbing a jacket.

Rita turned to face me. Her long lashes had a few small snowflakes clinging to them. "I don't really want to talk to anyone about this, but I know Jett will keep stopping by until I do."

"Why don't you want to talk to him?"

She rolled her eyes. "Jett was a few years younger than me in school. I'm sure he's a great sheriff, but it's weird to think of him as someone with authority. I still remember when he put ketchup packets under the toilet seats when he was fourteen."

I tried not to smile. "That's fair."

"Look, I really don't want to talk about the night Tabitha died, but I will if you leave me alone once I tell you what I know."

"Alright." I folded my arms for warmth and tried not to let my teeth chatter.

"The day we were on the boat was awful. Our entire boat was full of people who hated Tabitha, and I understood why. She'd done at least one awful thing to everyone there."

"Including you?"

She shrugged. "She wasn't awful to Amy and me, but it was terrible spending time with her."

"Amy said she was only friends with her because she was scared of what would happen if she wasn't."

Rita let out a breath, and I could see it in the cold air. "That was the same with me. Tabitha was beautiful, and she had a dominant personality. She drew people to her and repulsed them at the same time. It's hard to describe someone like her. She messed up a lot of people's lives with her last scheme."

"So everyone had a motive to kill her."

"I think so."

I was having trouble keeping the chattering from my teeth. "So who killed her?"

She looked at the ground. "That night, I went out onto the deck with Tabitha. She wanted to be out there but was scared of the dark. She never said that, but I could tell. Well, she started ranting about everyone on the boat and how unfair it was that we were all put together. Everyone hated her, and she knew it. She didn't mind being hated, but being stuck with everyone made her uncomfortable. She was also upset about Jack."

"Because he broke up with her?"

"Yes. That and he was really mad at her. Jack isn't someone you want to upset. He can get a little scary. He'd lost money, and he wasn't happy."

"Everyone thinks she pocketed their money."

"I'm almost sure she did."

"But you and Amy didn't lose anything?"

"No. I didn't have any money to invest, or I'm sure she would have manipulated me somehow. Amy usually let Tabitha push her around, but she'd refused to invest."

I nodded. "What did she say that night?"

"She was complaining about how unfair it was that people hated her. She said people should have known there was a risk when they invested and shouldn't blame her. Jack's name came up more than once. Tabitha dated almost every guy in our grade, but the only one she really liked was Jack. I don't know why she didn't just give him his money back."

"Was that why he broke up with her?"

"No. He broke up with her before everything went down. He invested with her after they broke up. I don't actually know what happened. I just know they had a huge fight. I think there was too much vanity from both sides of the relationship, and it was doomed to fail."

"So Jack was good-looking?"

"He was. Not enough to get crazy about, though. They were a great-looking couple, but they both wanted to be the alpha. I think that was the problem."

I wondered if my nose was turning blue. It was so cold. "So who killed her?"

"It was late while she vented to me. I wanted to go to bed because we had had a busy day. Peter came out and said he needed to talk to Tabitha. I was only too happy to excuse myself. I walked around to the other side of the boat. Before I could go inside, I heard a splash."

"So you think Peter killed her?"

"That's my guess. What else could it have been? He was the last person with her."

"You didn't go see what caused the splash?"

She arched her brow. "No. It was dark. I figured it was a big fish. I went to bed. Wouldn't you?"

I thought about it for a moment. Honestly, I didn't know. I don't think I would have gone to bed. I would have peeked around the corner in the least, but maybe Rita wasn't as nosy as I was. "Did you tell anyone?"

"No. When the police questioned us, I didn't think it was important. It was a splash. I could have been wrong, and I wasn't going to blame poor Peter. It's terrible that it happened, but she had it coming. She treated Peter terribly."

"Why are you telling me now?"

"Because I know you aren't going to let it go like the police. They decided it was an accident pretty fast. I just want to clear myself and move on. Now that you know who did it, you can figure the rest out, and everything can return to normal."

"Thanks for talking to me. Do you want to come in for dinner?"

"No, I have family over, then I'm leaving for a while. I'll come back when everything is out in the open, and it's not dangerous."

"I don't think anything is dangerous right now."

"Peter isn't a bad guy, but guilt does weird things to people. I don't want to be around if he gets angry. I ratted him out. Good luck with everything." She turned and bounded off into the snow.

I went back into the diner and back to my seat. Jett and his parents were watching me expectantly. I rubbed my arms. "It's cold out there."

"Is the case solved?" Carol asked. "Did Rita know who killed Tabitha?"

I sighed. "She has a guess that sounds promising. I wouldn't say it's hard evidence."

"We can talk about it later," Jett said. "It's been ten years. Another half hour won't change anything."

Carol shook her head and looked at her husband. "That's Jett's way of saying this isn't our business."

Tanner chuckled. "And it's not. I'm sure we'll hear about it when it's all wrapped up."

I took a bite of room-temperature potatoes and cringed.

Carol tapped a finger against her lip. "I wonder why Rita didn't want to talk to Jett."

I smiled. "Something about ketchup packets under toilet seats."

Jett grinned. "Man. I didn't think anyone knew that was me. She can't hold that against me. It was a long time ago."

Carol frowned. "You did that? That's awful."

"I was like, thirteen or something. Teenagers do dumb things."

"That doesn't make it alright."

"Yes, Mom."

"I hope you apologized to anyone who might have been upset by your prank."

"Mom, it was so long ago. I don't even know who might have sat on it."

"Well, you should make a public apology. You can't hold a position of authority in a town where you performed such a tasteless prank."

I smiled as I imagined Jett standing on a table and apologizing to all the people.

"What are you grinning about?" Jett asked, bumping me with his shoulder.

"Nothing," I said. "I'm going to let you talk to your mom while I microwave my food." I grabbed my plate and went into the kitchen. A small circle of people stood in the back talking to José. I didn't have to worry about him being lonely back here. I slid my plate in the microwave and pushed the button.

People were still conversing and looked to be having a good time. I had worried Rita's announcement would ruin the mood. I pulled out my plate and went back to the Malones. Carol still looked annoyed, and Jett and his dad were laughing about something.

I scooted back in next to Jett. "Sorry, I hate room-temperature food."

Jett grinned. "I'm almost ready for pie."

I looked at his empty plate. "Didn't you take time to taste it?"

He laughed. "I did, and it was great. You and José did a great job."

"It was all José. I only helped with the pie, but not the hard ones."

Carol's frown faded away. "I hate cooking. I was thrilled when Jett told me you were doing Thanksgiving here."

"I'm glad you could come." I took a bite of turkey. José really had outdone himself.

Jett stood, and I got out of the booth so he could pass. "Does anyone want me to grab them some pie?"

Carol shook her head. "I'm still working on my food."

I shook my head since my mouth was full.

Tanner got up. "I'll come with you."

I smiled as I watched them walk away. Jett had a nice family.

Chapter 16

I sat on my bed with my back up against the headboard. I held *War and Peace* in my hands and began going through it page by page. The number 7 was written in the corner of the first page. Creepers slept next to me. I'd overeaten and wasn't going to be able to sleep, so I might as well do something useful. I meticulously checked every margin, but I wasn't coming up with anything so far.

Why did the book have to be this big? I tried to focus, but my mind kept going back to Thanksgiving dinner. It had been so much better than I'd imagined. I think everyone left happy and full. Jett had eaten four pieces of pie and would be useless tomorrow. If he could sleep after all that food, I would be shocked.

I was about to turn a page when something caught my eye. I turned back and smiled. One word had a circle around the letter U. I grabbed a notepad from my nightstand and wrote U. I ripped a sheet from it and tore it into strips, sticking one piece in to mark the page. I didn't want to lose it just in case I wanted to come back.

I felt a fresh surge of energy as I went through the pages, scanning for more circled letters. Each time I found one, I wrote it down. By the time I got to the last page, I had eight letters. U, T, S, P, A, D, E.

The clock read 1:59 a.m. I couldn't call anyone. They would be as clueless as I was, so waking someone wouldn't do any good. I started unscrambling letters to make words. Pushed, pad, shut, tad, spat, date, pest, spa. This wasn't going to help. I grabbed my phone and downloaded an app that unscrambled words. The only word that used every letter was *updates*.

I sighed. What could any of this mean? Would it really hurt to text Jett? If he was sleeping, he wouldn't see it until morning. Right as I was about to tap Jett's number on my phone, it rang and made me jump. Jett had beat me to it. I answered.

"Hello?"

"Hey, Ivy. You awake?"

"Nope, how about you?"

He chuckled. "I mean, did I wake you?"

"No. I was just about to text you."

"Oh? Why?"

"I found something in the book but can't make sense of it."

"You still didn't tell me what Rita said either."

I shifted, and Creepers batted at me. "Is that why you called?"

"Yeah. I was going to stay after dinner and talk then, but you got really busy. Can I come over?"

"It's the middle of the night."

"But we're both up."

"I guess."

"I'll be over in a few."

His phone clicked, and I jumped out of bed. Creepers gave me an annoyed meow and hopped to the floor. I grabbed some clean clothes and changed from my pajamas. I ran a brush through my hair and brushed my teeth even though I already had before bed. It was ridiculous, and I knew it, but I wasn't chancing bad breath when Jett was here.

There was a knock on my bedroom door, and I froze. No one should be able to get in the diner. My eyes flew across the room as I looked for a weapon. Why didn't I have anything?

"Ivy?" Jett said from behind the door.

I opened the door. "You freaked me out! How did you get in here?"

"The front door wasn't locked."

I let out a slow breath. "I guess I got distracted after doing all the dishes after dinner."

Jett pointed at the book on my messy bed. "So what's in the book?"

I grabbed it and handed it to him. It had several small ripped-up pieces of paper marking all the letters I'd found. "There are letters in the book that are circled. I've been trying to unscramble them, but I'm not getting anywhere."

He opened the book to one page I'd marked. "I think there are some online resources that can unscramble things."

"I tried. The only word that uses all the letters is updates. Do you think that means anything?"

He frowned and handed the book back. "Nothing I can think of. What did Rita say?"

"She thinks it was Peter. I've never met him, so I don't have an opinion."

Jett sat on the window seat. "I find that hard to believe. Peter isn't my favorite person or anything, but I don't think he's a killer."

I sat across from him at the foot of my bed. "What if he was really mad and just pushed her in an angry moment?"

"I guess that's possible. Why does she think it was him?"

"She said she was out on the deck with Tabitha, and Peter came out and wanted to talk to Tabitha. Rita walked around the boat, and she heard a splash."

"Why didn't she tell anyone?"

I shrugged. "She said she didn't want Peter to get in trouble."

"Hmm. I'll go talk to him in the morning."

Creepers jumped up next to Jett and meowed at him.

I smiled. "I think you're in his space."

"Sorry," he said, standing. Creepers rolled up where Jett had been sitting, and Jett sat beside me on the bed.

He picked up the book I had dumped on the bed and started looking through it. "Could you have missed any letters?"

"It's possible. My mind was wandering when I first started going through it. If I missed something, it's probably toward the front."

We sat in silence while Jett turned the pages slowly. My eyelids were getting heavy, and I struggled to keep them open.

"Here," he said, making me jump. "There is an H right here." I looked at the spot he was pointing.

I grabbed my notepad and wrote an H. "Great. Now we have H, U, T, S, P, A, D, E."

"Hut spade?"

I nodded. "That doesn't make any more sense than updates."

"Maybe there is a hut, and we need to take a spade and dig something up?"

I frowned. "That doesn't sound promising. Do you know of any huts around here?"

"No."

"I don't think I can think about this anymore tonight. My eyes are burning."

"Really? I'm feeling more awake than ever. And I can't stop thinking about all the leftover pie that must be in the kitchen."

I tilted my head. "Please tell me you're joking? You had four pieces."

He grinned as he stood. "That was hours ago."

"Fine. I'll get you some pie." He grabbed my hands and pulled me to my feet.

"José should win a prize for making the best pie. You only ate one piece."

"I'm more of a cookie person."

"And your cookies are great."

It took me until we were halfway to the kitchen to realize Jett was holding my hand. I wondered if he was aware. We went into the kitchen, and I dropped his hand. I didn't want to, but I was tired, and now wasn't the time to fixate on something like this.

"What kind do you want? We overestimated how many pies we would need, so you can take one."

"My own pie? Nice. Do you have pumpkin?"

"Yep." I pulled open the fridge and grabbed one. They weren't going to stay good for long. It might be a good idea to try to sell them tomorrow. "Here you go."

He took it. "Thanks. I should go. I'll come find you tomorrow after I talk to Peter."

I nodded. "Sounds good. I'll walk you to the door and make sure I lock it this time." I followed him out of the kitchen and into the dining area. The tiredness had caught up to me. I was going to fall asleep as soon as my head hit the pillow.

Jett pushed open the door and grinned. "Thanks again for the pie."

I watched him walk out into the dark night. I shut the door and locked it, then I checked the back door just to be safe. My mind went to Jett holding my hand, and I pushed the thought away. Focusing on the mystery was a better use of time. We were getting close. I could feel it. A few more days and we might be there.

Chapter 17

José, Boyd, and I sat in a booth looking over my notes from last night. The diner was slow this morning. Everyone must be recovering from Thanksgiving dinner.

"The letters can be unscrambled to say dustheap," Boyd said.

I laughed. "Dustheap makes no more sense than hut spade."

José rested his chin on his hand while he studied the letters. "I wonder if Jett was right. Maybe we are supposed to get a spade and dig by a hut."

"Where do we find a hut?" I asked.

"No idea. Maybe it's not a hut. Maybe it's the trailer in the woods."

Boyd shook his head. "Nah. Then the clue would have been trailer spade. No one is going to mistake a trailer for a hut."

"I'm a little nervous if we are supposed to dig something up."

José nodded. "I would be, but there isn't a missing body, so we wouldn't have to worry about that turning up."

"So what do we do? If we don't have a hut, I'm not sure what our next move should be." I'd been thinking about it from the moment I woke up. Why couldn't it be another book clue? Stan was really making this annoying. He was probably laughing at us from the other side.

José scratched his head. "When is Jett talking to Peter? If he confesses, we can be finished with the clues."

Boyd shook his head. "I can't believe that from Peter."

"I don't know," José said. "If I remember right, Peter ended a relationship for Tabitha, then she dumped him a month later. Then he made the stupid mistake of investing with her and lost a lot of money. It's an excellent motive."

"Yes, but almost everyone on the boat had as good of a motive or better. I would look into Rita. She's the one suddenly pointing her finger and trying to get people to stay away from her."

I bit the inside of my cheek. "What would she have to gain from Tabitha's death? They were friends, and she didn't lose any money."

"Yes, but Tabitha was always bossing Rita and Amy around. They couldn't make a life's choice without consulting her. I'm sure they were ready to be rid of her."

I rested my elbows on the table and ran my hands through my hair. "Too many people are involved. With the last two cases, I could keep my head wrapped around things. This time, it's hard to remember what I'm thinking from day to day."

My phone buzzed, and I pulled it from my pocket. I had a text message from Jett. "Jett can't go talk to Peter today. He's busy with a domestic dispute."

"We could go," Boyd offered.

"I should stay here," José stated. "Things might pick up by lunch. The two of you should go, though."

"Are you sure?" I asked.

"Yes."

I glanced at my watch. "We better do it early. I need to go help Barbra later today."

José chuckled. "More cleaning?"

"Yep. It might take years."

"Well, you're a good friend. Don't worry about the diner. I have everything under control."

Boyd and I drove over to Peter's house. He lived on a farm just outside town.

"Won't he be working?" I asked. "It isn't even noon yet."

"He doesn't have a job outside his farm," Boyd said. "That means even if he's working, he'll be close to home because it isn't harvest season. All he has to do is take care of his animals."

I followed Boyd's instructions and ended up in front of a two-story farmhouse. If Peter was still suffering from Tabitha's scheme, it didn't show. The house was large and well-kept. We parked and stood looking up at the house.

"Even if he isn't home, his wife probably knows where he is," Boyd said.

"He's married?"

"Yep. He's been married for about five years. He has a two or three-year-old."

We walked up to the door and rang the bell. No one answered.

"Let's go check the barn," Boyd suggested. I followed him around the house and over to a large brown barn. The door was opened a crack. Boyd pushed it open and yelled, "Hello in here! It's Boyd."

"In the back," a deep voice said. I followed Boyd into the structure and past stalls full of cows. When we got to the last stall, we saw a man bending down, holding a brown chick in a bowl of water.

My eyes narrowed. "What are you doing?"

The man looked up, startled. "You aren't Boyd."

"I'm here," Boyd said, appearing at my side. "This is Ivy Clark. I don't think you've met."

"Hello," he said, keeping his grip on the chick.

"Are you giving it a bath?" I asked. "It seems cold for that."

The man sighed. "The water is warm. We had a hidden clutch of eggs. They hatched, and it's not really the best season for that. We have to work harder on keeping them warm."

"How does holding them in water help? Won't that make them colder once you take them out?"

Boyd chuckled. "Sometimes chicks get poop stuck to their little fannies. It can be dangerous, so you have to clean it off."

Peter nodded. "Exactly. This little guy has needed to be cleaned twice already."

"Won't he be too cold?" I asked. The barn wasn't windy, but it was still almost as cold as outside.

"I'll dry him off and put him under warm lights. What can I do for you? I'm pretty sure you didn't come by to worry about my chicks."

Boyd chuckled. "We came to ask you if you killed Tabitha Coats." I shot Boyd a look. Didn't he know how to be subtle?

Peter grabbed a clean rag and gently cleaned the chicken. He didn't seem surprised or concerned by Boyd's question. "Nope. Sorry."

"I didn't think so," Boyd said.

I stepped closer to the enclosure. "Someone said that you might have."

He looked up but still didn't look surprised. "Oh? Was it Jana White? She has plenty of reasons to hate me."

"No. Someone said you were talking to her that night, and then they heard a big splash." I wondered who Jana White was. Perhaps the girl he'd left when he started dating Tabitha.

His brows came together. "I talked to her, but there was no splash. Not while I was there."

"Why were you talking to her?"

"I assume you know about Tabitha tricking everyone and taking their money?"

"Yes."

"Well, I was pretty sure she had pocketed all the money. I told her I was having someone look into it if she didn't come clean and return the money. She just smirked and told me to get lost. I heard someone coming from the other way. I didn't want to air my problems out for everyone, so I left."

"Did you hear a splash?"

"No, but I heard her greet someone. And no, I don't know who it was. It was a man, that's all I know. I was mad and not concentrating on it."

I leaned against one stall. "So you have no idea who might have killed her."

He stood with the chick and snuggled it close to him. He swallowed hard and then took a deep breath. "Sometimes I wonder if she jumped. I've felt guilty about it for years.

Maybe when I told her I was going to get the authorities involved, she freaked out."

"I don't think so," I told him. I didn't want to tell him about the clues in the books and the man in the woods, but I didn't want him to feel guilty if he didn't need to. "We are pretty sure someone was behind it."

"You'll probably never figure it out. Everyone on that boat had a reason to want her out of the way. It's been so long. I don't think you will find any evidence."

"There may have been a witness," Boyd said. "Just give us a call if you ever think of anything, alright?"

"Sure thing."

We went back to my car and climbed in. "I don't think he did it," I said as we pulled away from the house.

"That's what I've been saying."

"This is so frustrating. I wish we could figure out what the hut and spade mean."

"Could it be a book reference? Everything else has been."

I rubbed my lips together. "I guess so, but nothing obvious comes to mind."

"I'll look on my phone," Boyd said, pulling it out of his pocket. "Huts and spades and books," he muttered to himself.

I waited for a few minutes so he could search. "Did anything come up?"

"Just a bunch of kid's books and stuff. Nothing useful."

"I should go ask Brian. He's the expert."

"Good idea. I'm going to ask around about huts. If there are any around these parts, I don't know of them, but maybe someone else does."

"I wonder if we're missing something obvious." This last clue was really throwing me. We could be interpreting it all wrong. Perhaps the letters stood for something and weren't meant to be words at all. Unscrambling them could mean anything.

I didn't have much time today. I still needed to go help Barbra. It sounded like Jett was busy, so I couldn't use his truck. I could either take a smaller load or make a pile for Jett to pick up later.

Since Barbra doesn't want to watch me clean, I should have plenty of time to think.

Chapter 18

"I don't want the things in this wardrobe to be thrown away," Barbra said, pointing at a large oak wardrobe. It was intricately carved with small designs and looked like it needed to be refinished. I hadn't noticed it because of all the other things in the room.

"What's in it?" I asked.

Barbra shrugged and pushed her newly orange hair over her shoulder. "I haven't gotten around to going through it. I got it at an estate sale years ago."

"And you haven't looked inside?"

"I glanced in there when I got it home. Getting it here wasn't an easy feat. We had to tie it together so it wouldn't come open, and it took Jett and four others to get it in here. It's stuffed full of things."

"Why would someone sell something without cleaning it out first?"

"I got it from the Clements Manor. Have you seen it?"

"No."

"It's the biggest home around these parts. You have to go out of your way to get there. It's hidden behind enormous trees. Once you get down the long driveway, an immense mansion comes into view. The Clements have lived there for over a hundred years."

"I've never heard of them."

"The family keeps away from this town. They are ridiculously wealthy. They have staff who come into town. I think when they do their business, they prefer going to Wichita. They have big parties, but no one around here has ever been to one."

"I'm surprised no one talks about them. It sounds mysterious."

"Zeb Clements was the grandfather. When he died, they sold almost everything and redecorated. I got the wardrobe almost like a surprise box. I paid and got to keep everything inside. It sounded like a fun mystery at the time, but by the time we got it in here, I wasn't in the mood to sift through someone else's junk. I keep putting it off, but I'll get to it someday."

The hairs on my arms stood up at the thought of what that could contain. "When you go through it, can I be here? I would love to see what's inside."

"I would love nothing more. We can do it once all this garbage is out of the way."

I smiled so big it hurt. "That will motivate me to get through this stuff faster."

Barbra patted my hand. "I would hate to see what happened to your wallet if you ever went to an estate sale."

I laughed. "I should probably stay away from things like that."

"How goes the hunt for Tabitha's killer?"

I opened a box full of used wrapping paper. "I'm a little stuck. We found a clue in a book that said hut spade. Or if you unscramble it—dustheap."

"Could something be buried near a hut and you have to use a spade to find it?"

"We thought about that, but no one can think of a place with a hut."

Barbra leaned against the wall and looked up at the ceiling. "Let's think. Something could be hidden in a dustheap."

"Any ideas of where we would find one? Especially one that would still be around ten years later."

"Not really. You are stuck. I'll keep thinking about it and tell you if I come up with something. You're going to throw away all my old wrapping paper, aren't you?"

I grinned. "Probably."

"Then I'm going upstairs so I don't have to see it. Call for me if you need me."

"Alright." I grabbed the box and took it out to my car. I wasn't going to make much progress today. My car had a nice hatchback but not a ton of space. I decided to only take garbage today. With any luck, I could fit the stuff in the big bin behind the diner.

As soon as I finished at Barbra's, I stopped at the diner to dump the garbage, then went inside to grab something to eat. Boyd sat on the floor in the corner of the lobby with Creepers.

"Hey, Boyd," I said, squatting near him. "What are you doing?"

"I'm trying to see how smart a cat is," he said, holding up a laser pointer. "I was just thinking, they have dogs trained to help police, but what if we train Creepers?" Creepers was clawing his way up Boyd's shirt.

I arched my brow. "Train a cat to help with our cases? I'm not seeing it."

"They have dogs that can sniff out drugs. Cats have a good sense of smell, so why not let them do the same? Or teach them to sniff out dead bodies? I think I'm onto something."

I smiled. "Creepers enjoys eating and sitting in the window. I don't see him getting drug-sniffing motivation."

"You don't think he can do it?"

I tilted my head and watched Creepers fall over Boyd's shoulder. "Even if he could, I don't think he would. He does his own thing."

"Well, I don't think we should rule it out. Can I try?"

"To train my cat to sniff out drugs? How are you going to do that?"

"I'll do an internet search. It's amazing what you can find on there."

I stood upright and crossed my arms. "Training a dog might be easier. Why don't you get a dog?"

Creepers crawled back onto Boyd's lap, and he rubbed his fur. "I love dogs, but I don't have the energy for one. Just give me a week to prove I can do it."

I shrugged. "Alright, but don't be disappointed if it doesn't work. I'm going over to the library if you need anything."

"I might need a hand up. Seventy-year-old people should not sit on the floor."

I laughed and turned to the occupied tables. "Can someone help me get Boyd off the floor?"

A smiling man stood and came to our aid. We got Boyd to his feet. He brushed off his pants and sighed. "I remember when that was a simple thing."

I grabbed a banana from the kitchen and pulled on my coat. There was no point in driving to the library when it was so close. The air was chilly, but it wasn't snowing. I passed by all the small shops on the square and turned the corner. My mind was full of so many thoughts. I went into the library, but Brian wasn't at his desk.

I wandered past the aisles until I found him putting books away in the children's section.

"Hi, Brian."

"Hey, Ivy. What's happening?"

"I found a clue in *War and Peace*, but we are completely baffled by it."

He clasped his hands together and smiled. "Throw it at me."

"Letters in the book were circled. If we look at them in order, they say hut spade."

He rubbed his hands together. "Hmm. That's a tough one. Could it be a book with a hut on the cover?"

"Maybe. We tried searching on the internet but didn't come up with anything. We were thinking we might need a shovel to dig something up. Are there books with huts on the covers?"

"Sure. I'm trying to think." He walked to another shelf and pulled out a children's book. It had a hut and a tree on it. Nothing about a spade. He handed it to me, and I went and sat on a large stuffed chair. I turned the pages slowly, looking for anything that might be a clue. "I doubt that's the right one. I don't think that book has existed for more than a few years."

"I'm going to look, just in case."

"I'll try to find more books."

Brian disappeared around a shelf, and I kept looking at the book. It only had thirty-three pages, so it didn't take me long to see there was nothing there. I closed the book and went to return it to its shelf. A little girl and her mom were looking at the shelf, so I waited off to the side until they were finished, and then I put the book away.

I wandered around for a few minutes, looking at books but not taking any off the shelf. I didn't have time to read until I solved Tabitha's murder.

"There you are," Brian said. I turned to see him standing in front of me with a huge grin on his face. He held his hands behind him.

"Did you find anything?" I asked eagerly.

"I think so." He pulled a book out and handed it to me. The cover had two huts on it.

I looked at the title. "*The No. 1 Ladies' Detective Agency*. It does have a hut."

"And look at the hut," he said, pointing at a shape on the hut next to the door.

"It looks like a shape from a playing card." I didn't play cards, so I wasn't exactly sure. "A spade? Is that what it's called?"

Brian looked at me and nodded. "And that would mean…"

"Oh! A hut and a spade!" I jumped up and down. "Brian, you are the best!" I gave him a hug, and he laughed. "I never would have guessed something like that."

"I'm glad I could help."

“Okay, okay. I’m going to sit in the corner and look through the book. If I go back to the diner, I’ll get distracted.”

“It stays pretty quiet here. Let me know if you need anything.”

“Thanks.” I went back to the cushy chair and sat down. I looked at the first and last pages. On the first page was a number 32 written in blue ink. I flipped to page thirty-two, but nothing stood out. Two of the other books also had numbers, but I hadn’t focused on them.

The book must have been donated from another library. It had a card in the back from when the librarian would write your name on it when you checked it out. I pulled it out. It had a few names on it. After the names, someone had written *justice served* in blue pen.

My heart began pounding. I hoped that wasn’t the end of the clue. That sounded harder than *hut spade*. I flipped through the book quickly, and then again a bit slower. Something caught my eye, and I went back a few pages. Someone had circled a name. Jack.

Chapter 19

I paced the empty diner while José and Boyd sat at a booth looking at the book.

Boyd looked up at me. "It seems pretty clear. Jack McBride did it."

"But why does it say justice served?" I asked. "That's the thing that bothers me."

José turned to the last page and pulled out the card. "What if this is the last book? The justice served is because we got to the end, and now Jack can be punished."

"I suppose that could be right. That still leaves problems. Like where is Jack? And some cryptic clues in some books don't make a person guilty. It's far from hard evidence."

"So what do we do?" José asked.

"I'm not sure. I'll take any ideas you two have."

Boyd leaned against his seat. "I've got nothing. I think we need to find Jack and get him to confess."

"Jett's been trying to find him. If he can't, I'm not sure we can. He has a lot more resources than we do."

José held up the book. "Have you shown this to Jett?"

"Not yet. I haven't seen him today." I moved when Creepers went shooting across the room. He gets hyper before bed.

Someone pounded on the diner door.

"I got it," José said, jumping up and rushing to the door. "It's Brian." He opened the door, and Brian came in. He wore a blue puffy coat and a matching beanie. In his hand, he held a book.

"We had an anonymous donation of books today," he said. "They came in the mail."

"Oh?"

"There was a book I thought you might want to see." He held it out. On the cover was a gravestone and written across the stone in Sharpie, it said, "Justice is here."

I grabbed the book and stared at it. "The handwriting looks about the same. Why would it come to you now? It doesn't make any sense. Stan could have had someone mail a book to you at some later date, but there is no way he would know to do it now." I'd never heard of the book. I opened it to the copyright page. "This book was published last year."

Boyd frowned. "What does this mean?"

I tapped the book against my leg. "Either Stan isn't the one who wrote the notes or he isn't dead."

Brian sat at a table. "Did anyone else just get a chill running over their spine?" José raised his hand.

"Stan's cousin Tyson said he buried Stan himself. If Stan isn't dead, then Tyson lied."

Boyd stood. "Let's go dig up the grave."

I wrinkled my nose. "That sounds hard and disgusting. It's been nine years. If Stan was still around, wouldn't someone have noticed?"

Boyd zipped up his coat. "What if Stan is the one who tied me up in the woods?"

José nodded. "Perhaps Stan thought he was so clever he would hang around and see how it all played out."

"Why pretend to be dead?" I asked.

Brian slapped the table. "If he's dead, no one can bother him. If people were looking for a killer, he couldn't just say, 'Oh, you'll find out if you play my game.' The police wouldn't go for that."

My gaze fell across each of them. All three of them had shiny eyes. "You all really want to go dig up a grave? We should probably go find Jett."

Boyd shook his head. "Jett's a good kid, but if we tell him, then we have to go by his rules. He'll have to get permission to dig up the grave."

"What if the grave has nothing to do with anything?"

Boyd grinned. "Then we'll apologize to his corpse, cover him back up, and plant some nice flowers for him in the spring."

I smiled and shook my head. "You know Jett's going to get mad."

"You can blame it all on me. I'm an old guy. What's he going to do?"

"Where are we going to get some shovels?"

"I have plenty at my place," Boyd said.

"It's freezing outside. Won't the ground be frozen?"

Boyd nodded. "Sure will. I have a pickaxe. That might work better than a shovel. We better get started."

"I have some big lanterns we can take," Brian offered. "They are pretty nice. They'll light up a big area."

Boyd clapped him on the back. "Glad to have you with us."

We filed out to my car. I couldn't believe I was agreeing to this. I'm okay with breaking some rules in the name of justice, but this is almost too much for me.

Brian got in the front, and José and Boyd got in the back. We stopped at Brian's for the lanterns and then at Boyd's for the shovels and pickaxe. They barely fit in the back of the car.

"Let me grab something from inside," Boyd said, running into his house. We waited a few minutes, and he came running back out. He had a pile of logs in his arms and a grocery bag hanging from his elbow. He climbed in and dumped the logs on the floor by his feet.

José looked at the floorboard. "What's that for?"

"I had an idea. We make a fire first. That will help thaw the ground."

I drove down the road, a fight going on inside me. Jett was going to be annoyed when he found out we did this. There was probably a law against it. I wasn't going to look it up to see. If we knew there was a law, we might get in more trouble than if we didn't.

I turned onto the cemetery road. "What if the person who tied up Boyd is still out in the woods watching things? We don't have any weapons."

José leaned forward. "Why is that? We keep ending up in strange situations. We should probably have something for protection."

"I'm not worried," Boyd said. "We have shovels."

I pulled into the small parking lot and killed the engine. We got out and waited for Brian to get the lanterns. He handed one to each of us. They were so bright, I couldn't look at mine. We went over to Stan's grave and set the lanterns around his tombstone.

Boyd dumped his logs on the ground and pulled out a lighter.

"Whoa," Brian said, pushing down Boyd's arm. "First, we need to clear the area of weeds so the fire doesn't spread."

"The weeds are wet and dead. I don't think they're a fire hazard," Boyd protested.

"We're cleaning the area," Brian said. He began tearing away weeds growing by the gravestone. The rest of us joined in. When Brian decided it was clear enough, Boyd started a fire.

I looked back into the trees. All I could see was darkness. "I bet it's illegal to start a fire in a cemetery."

Boyd laughed. "Probably not as illegal as digging up a grave."

"How long do we let the fire burn?"

Boyd shrugged and held up his grocery bag. "Long enough to make some s'mores."

I rolled my eyes. "I'm not making s'mores over a grave."

Boyd shrugged. "That's fine by me." He pulled out some roasting sticks and marshmallows.

"You're really going to do it?" Brian asked.

Boyd shrugged. "Not if it's going to make you all squeamish." He put the stuff back in the bag and went and put it in the car. I wanted to sit and wait for the fire to do its thing, but the ground would be too cold to sit on.

"How long do we wait?" I asked.

José shrugged. "I don't know. It's cold out here, but I don't think the ground is too frozen. We've only had light snow, and none of it has stayed around for more than a day."

I grabbed a shovel and went far from the fire. I tried to dig the shovel into the earth, jumping on it. It went in about an inch. I sighed. This was going to take forever. I'd dug with Boyd and José before, and Boyd only had about ten minutes in him before his back couldn't take it.

After what felt like forever, Boyd put out the fire. He lit another one a few feet away, so we started digging where the first fire had been. Brian and José were doing alright. I was making a bit of progress, and Boyd was struggling. I didn't think the fire had done any good. José grabbed the pickaxe, which worked better than the shovels.

"Six feet down, right?" I asked after fifteen minutes.

José looked up. "That's what they say."

"Don't hurt yourself, Boyd," Brian said. "We would rather you sit and watch than throw your back out."

"Sorry," Boyd said, wiping his brow. "Getting old is the worst." He put his shovel down and looked up at the sky. "What are the chances we get this all done and then covered up again by morning?"

"We're making progress," José said. The pickaxe hit something. "That can't be it already."

"If it is, it's not buried deep enough," Brian said. We started concentrating on that area.

"I can see the headlines tomorrow," Boyd said. "Local librarian, diner owner, cook, and retired old guy dig up grave."

"What did you retire from?" I asked Boyd.

He laughed. "I did it all, but mostly farming."

"And that made enough money to retire?"

"My parents are probably rolling in their graves, but I sold off all the farmland and only kept the house. It has me set for the rest of my life."

"Shine a light over here," Brian said. Boyd turned on his phone's flashlight and shined it into the hole. "That looks like a coffin."

I pushed my hair behind my ear and looked down at the wood we were uncovering. "Why is it so shallow? I wonder if we should leave it and call Jett. We should talk to Stan's cousin Tyson."

"You aren't getting squeamish, are you?" Boyd teased.

"I'm just thinking about how much trouble we might get into." It wasn't a lie. I really was worried. I was also nervous about opening a grave. We kept working until we had most of the dirt off the top and down part of the sides. My shoulders were killing me.

"We don't need to unearth the entire thing," I said. "We should be able to open it now and look in."

"Let's do it," José said.

I took a deep breath. "I don't want to be a wimp, but this could ruin my sleep for the rest of my life."

"We can get it," José said. "You can stay back."

Brian shot José a half grin. "What about my dreams?"

They both bent down and fiddled with something. I heard a click, and then Brian and José lifted the lid.

All I could see was the lid, and I didn't want to see more.

Brian's brows came together, and José frowned.

"Well," Boyd asked. "Is there a body?"

"Yes," Brian said, "but I don't think it's Stan."

"No," José agreed. "Look at that belt buckle. I'd know it anywhere. This is Jack McBride."

Chapter 20

I sat in my car with my phone at my ear. It rang three times before Jett answered.

"Hello?" he said groggily.

"Jett? It's Ivy. We have a... situation."

He sighed. "It's three in the morning."

"We dug up Stan's grave."

Silence answered me.

"Jett?"

"I think I'm still dreaming. Did you just say you dug up Stan's grave?"

"Yes."

"That's against the law, Ivy."

"Well, don't you want to know what we found?" I asked.

"Stan's body, I presume."

"No."

"There wasn't a body?"

"There was, but not Stan's. José said it's Jack McBride."

"I'll be there as soon as I can." He hung up.

I got out of the car and walked back to the others. They stood around the coffin talking quietly.

"Jett's coming," I told them.

Boyd nodded. "Is he mad?"

"I'm not sure. He definitely wasn't happy."

"I guess we know why Jett couldn't find Jack now," José said. "Does that mean Stan is behind it all?"

I crossed my arms for warmth. "Maybe. The book said 'justice served.' It's possible Stan thought he saw Jack kill Tabitha, and then he killed Jack in the name of justice."

"I don't know," Brian said. "Stan was a little strange, but I didn't think of him as a killer."

I yawned. "We also need to think about Stan's cousin Tyson. He said Stan was dead. How could he be mistaken about something like this? He must have known Stan wasn't in the grave."

José's eyes went wide. "This grave was too shallow. What if someone buried Jack here after Stan's death? Stan could still be down there."

I shivered. "That sounds very possible."

We talked more until we saw Jett's truck pull up. He walked toward us, frowning. "I really wish you guys would leave all of this to the law."

I tilted my head. "Would you have dug up the grave?"

He sighed. "I don't know. But you shouldn't have." Kneeling, he lifted the coffin lid and grimaced. "Yep, that's definitely not Stan. It looks like it could be Jack, but we'll have to run some tests to confirm."

"It's Jack's belt buckle," Boyd said.

"Looks like it."

I wasn't going to look in. "Why does everyone know what Jack's belt buckle looks like?"

Boyd chuckled. "He used to make them himself. They were always big with his initials on them."

"You should all probably leave," Jett said. "I'll call in some officers from Wichita and get some things in motion."

I arched my brow. "Do you really want us to leave you alone in the dark, in a cemetery, with a body?"

Jett looked up at me. I couldn't read his expression. "I'll be fine."

"What are you going to do while you're waiting? Do they need to send people out this late? It's not like a fresh crime. It can probably wait until morning."

He sighed. "I'm sure it can, but I can't just leave an open grave."

"Well, I'm going to go wait in the car," Boyd said. "I'm too old to stay up this late."

José nodded. "Me too. I'll come with you."

Brian followed them. "I'll go with them to make sure they don't get into trouble." We watched the three of them walk to the parking area and get into my car.

Jett still looked irritated.

"I'm sorry we called you so late."

"You need to stop trying to do these things without me."

"I doubt you would have come with me if I'd told you."

"No, and I would have stopped you."

"That's what we figured."

He let out a slow breath. "I don't want you getting hurt. You aren't trained for these things."

"Did you notice how shallow the grave is?" I asked, trying to change the subject. "We were wondering if Stan might still be down there."

"We'll have to dig deeper and see. Well, not we. I'll have to have someone with better equipment than shovels come in and dig."

"Tyson Roberts seemed sure he'd buried his cousin here."

"He might have been lying."

"Do you think so? He seemed pretty annoyed by the engraving on Stan's tomb. Why lie for him?"

Jett shrugged. "There was something about him I didn't trust, but I can't exactly put my finger on it. First things first. We need to get this body to Wichita so they can identify him, then we need to dig deeper to see if Stan is under there. Once we know those two things, it will be easier to move on."

"Anything I can do?"

He raised one brow and crossed his arms. "Nothing. You need to leave this up to me. Trying to solve a possible mystery is one thing. Now that we know without a doubt something is going on, I can't have you interfering. I hope you don't get into trouble for digging this up."

I nodded. "I can *try* to stay out of it."

He groaned. "Ivy, this is under control. Let me do my thing, and I'll let you know how it goes."

"Fine." I didn't want to promise. There was no way I was going to rest until this was solved.

He yawned. "Why do you always have to do these things in the middle of the night?"

I grinned. "To be stealthy?"

He put his hands on my upper arms and peered down at me. "This is dangerous. We know there is someone out there who might cause harm to someone. Remember Boyd tied up in the woods? I want you to stay away from this area. Alright?"

"I have contractors coming soon. That might keep me busy."

"Good. Now, why don't you take your little posse home? I'm pretty sure it's past their bedtime. I bet they're all asleep in the car."

I narrowed my eyes. "I don't want to leave you here alone. Just because you're the sheriff doesn't mean someone can't hurt you or tie you up. We learned that a while back. You haven't forgotten, have you?"

He dropped my arms and sighed. "No, I haven't. You can stay in your car until I make a few calls, but then I want you to go. Alright?"

"I'll think about it." I went to my car and got in the driver's seat. No one was sleeping.

"That was disappointing," Boyd said. "I just lost five bucks."

I turned on the car and cranked up the heater. It was as cold here as outside. "What are you talking about?" I turned around to see Brian and José snickering in the back seat.

Boyd chuckled and held his hands in front of the heater. "I was sure Jett was going to kiss you out there. All he needed to do was move a few inches closer."

I forced a laugh. "Kiss me? He was telling me to stay out of his way."

"Really?" Brian asked. "That's not what it looked like from here. At least not during the part when he held your arms and looked dreamily into your eyes." The three of them burst into laughter.

I rolled my eyes. "I expect this from Boyd and José, but not you, Brian."

Boyd adjusted the heat vent. "We might be rubbing off on him."

I might occasionally daydream about Jett, but having him kiss me in front of these three would have been awful. I never would hear the end.

"So what now?" José asked.

"Jett wants us to stay out of everything. He wants us to leave him here so he can wait for some officers from Wichita to come."

Boyd shook his head. "He wants us to leave him alone in the dark cemetery? Doesn't he know there might be someone dangerous out here?"

I shrugged. "That's what I'm saying. We can leave once someone else comes. I don't care what he says—I'm not leaving him here."

Chapter 21

Two days later, I stood in the diner's kitchen, listening to the construction crew. Things were finally happening. It sounded like I could keep the diner open through most of the remodel. They were going to expand the building by going back first and then working on making the top floor larger. I couldn't wait to have a bigger living space.

I grated zucchini into a bowl and tried to keep my mind off whatever Jett was doing. The entire cemetery was now blocked off with crime scene tape, and I'm not brave enough to go under that. Jett puts up with a lot from me, but that might be pushing it.

The door to the kitchen swung open, and Livy entered. She was frowning and fiddling with her notepad.

"Hey, Livy. Is anything wrong?" I asked.

"There's a lawman here. He got really mad when I gave him his bill."

I raised an eyebrow. "Why? Our prices aren't bad."

"He said most restaurants give lawmen free food or at least half off the bill."

I rolled my eyes. "Don't worry, I'll talk to him." I went to the sink to wash my hands. Giving discounts to people didn't bother me, especially police and others who worked hard to keep things safe. What annoyed me was that this man thought it was owed to him.

"He's sitting at table two," Livy said.

I dried my hands on a dish towel. "Thanks."

I walked into the dining area and spotted a man in his mid-forties, with black hair and a mustache, sitting at table two. He was finishing a piece of pie.

A forced smile jumped to my face, and I approached him. "Hello. I'm Ivy Clark, the owner of the diner."

He looked me up and down and sneered. "Ivy? Isn't the diner called Sue's?"

"Sue was my grandma."

"Hmm. Well, Ivy Clark, your server says you don't have discounts for law enforcement."

I tried to think of the best way to respond. Jett always paid for his meals, but he got more than his fair share of free dessert. "I can take the pie off your bill."

He sniffed. "Sheriff Malone said this was an accommodating place to eat. I suppose I'll take the free pie if that's all you're going to offer."

I gave him a stiff smile. Giving him a free meal wouldn't hurt anything, but I didn't like something about him.

"I'm Deputy Sheriff Kaz Ledford. I wish I could say I'll be seeing you often, but not at your prices."

I clenched my teeth. "Are you here helping from Wichita?"

"No. I'll be working with Sheriff Malone. Of course, he doesn't have time to show me the ropes right now, so I'm just killing time."

Trying to force a smile after getting that answer was impossible. This man would be staying in town? Jett needed a deputy, but couldn't it be someone a little more pleasant?

"Well, come in for a free dessert whenever you have the time," I said. I hoped he wouldn't.

"I might. Does Sheriff Malone pay full price for his meals? He said he comes in a lot, but I can't imagine he can afford that on his salary."

"He pays full price. Except for dessert."

He took a sip of water. "You better hope no other restaurants move into town. They might be more competitive than you."

Before I had reopened the diner, José and I had researched prices at similar diners, and we were a little less than most of them. "I'll worry about that if it happens.

Muddy Creek is small and doesn't have a growing population."

The bell above the door tinkled, and Jett walked in. His hair was messy, and he looked tired. He spotted me talking to Deputy Ledford, and his frown went deeper. He walked toward us.

"Hello, Sheriff Malone," Deputy Ledford said. "Why don't you share my table? I'll get another dessert and keep you company." He grinned at me, and I gave him a tight smile.

"Thanks, Ledford." He sat across from the man. "Hi, Ivy. How's it going?"

"Great."

"I see the construction crew has started. That's exciting."

My eyes lit up. "Yes, I can't wait to see what they do."

"So that's why it's so loud," Deputy Ledford mumbled. "I'll have a brownie à la mode."

I nodded. "What can I get for you, Jett?"

He leaned back tiredly in his seat. "Can I get a burger and fries? Extra fries, if that's alright. I haven't eaten since yesterday."

I smiled. "You've got it."

Deputy Ledford crossed his arms. "You know she's going to charge you for the extra fries, right?"

Jett raised his brows. "Of course. Why wouldn't she?"

"I'm not going to charge you for extra fries," I said with my sweetest smile. "They'll be right out." I spun around and hurried to the kitchen before Deputy Ledford could respond. I grabbed Livy on my way and pulled her in with me.

"That man is the new deputy sheriff," I told her.

"Oh no! Does that mean he's going to live around here?"

"I'm afraid so. From now on, we are going to give free dessert to all emergency responders. Will you let the rest of the servers know?"

"Sure. I'm surprised that man was satisfied with that. I hate confrontations, and I think that guy enjoys them."

"He wanted more, but that's all I'm giving him. I think he might turn out to be a tremendous pain. I'm glad I'm not Jett. He's going to have to work with him every day."

José turned from where he was mixing something. "Jett finally has help? I bet that's nice for him."

"I hope so." I really did. Jett works too hard, but I had a feeling Deputy Ledford wasn't going to be the most pleasant person to work with. "Jett wants a burger and fries. Extra fries. The deputy wants a brownie à la mode. I have a feeling he'll be in here for a lot of free desserts."

One of the other cooks chuckled and shook his head. "It's not like Jett doesn't get a lot of free stuff."

"Yeah, but we like Jett," Livy said, straightening her red ponytail. "This guy is demanding." She turned and went back into the lobby. I was going to miss Livy when she went to college in January.

I peeked out the window and watched Jett and the new deputy. Jett kept yawning, and Deputy Ledford kept talking, his hands flying around as he spoke. He was passionate about whatever he was saying.

Once the food was ready, I grabbed the tray and took it out. I wasn't going to make one of the servers handle a difficult customer. I placed Jett's food in front of him and handed Deputy Ledford his brownie and ice cream.

"Thank you," Jett said, digging into his burger.

"Is there anything else I can get you?" I asked.

Deputy Ledford narrowed his eyes. "I was just telling the sheriff the importance of the way people perceive us. You should address him as Sheriff Malone, and you may call me Deputy Sheriff Ledford."

I raised my brow. "Deputy Sheriff Ledford. That's a mouthful."

The corners of Jett's mouth turned up as he chewed.

"But it's the appropriate way to address us."

Jett swallowed. "I don't mind if people call me by my first name. I grew up here, and I know everyone."

"How is your case coming?" I couldn't help asking.

"Fine. It would be better if I could get some sleep. We brought in an excavator and dug up the grave. No Stan."

"Interesting."

"You shouldn't be discussing this with civilians," Deputy Sheriff Ledford said. I definitely wasn't calling him that. It was too long.

Jett stuck a fry in his mouth. "Things are different in small towns. Ivy has helped a lot with the case I'm working, and no one would even be looking into it if it wasn't for her."

Deputy Ledford glared at me.

"The Wichita police don't want me talking to Tyson Roberts. They don't think he's relevant to anything."

I crossed my arms. "That doesn't make sense. He was either duped by Stan or part of his scheme. Someone needs to talk to him."

Jett winked at me. "I wish I could, but it's not in my jurisdiction, so there isn't a lot I can do."

I watched Jett's blank expression. Was he telling me to talk to Tyson? Even after he told me to stay out of things?

"I bet someone will look into it," I said.

"If they do, I hope they take Boyd."

I grinned. "I'm sure they will." I rushed to the kitchen and took off my apron. Everyone always wanted me to take Boyd. José would probably be more useful in a fight, but he was busy managing the diner.

"What's happening?" José asked.

I grabbed my phone and texted him.

He pulled out his phone and read the message. He nodded. "Take Boyd."

I rolled my eyes. "Of course."

Chapter 22

Boyd was nowhere to be found, so I was sitting by myself in Tyson Robert's office. I thought about asking Brian to come, but that would mean closing the library. Brian didn't employ anyone, so if he couldn't work, the library couldn't be open. A woman had shown me to the office, and I'd been waiting for over twenty minutes.

The door opened, and Mr. Roberts entered. When he saw me, he sighed. "Hello. Miss Clark, was it?"

I stood and shook his hand. "Yes. Thanks for seeing me."

"I didn't figure you would leave if I didn't. I've already told you everything I know about Stan's grave."

"Did you?" I asked, sitting when he did.

"What do you mean?"

"Stan's grave was dug up." I didn't tell him I helped do it.

"Why?" he asked. I wasn't positive, but he might have gone pale. "Do people really believe he knew something about Tabitha Coats? He was guessing, and nothing in the grave would help."

"Stan wasn't in the grave."

He blinked. "That's nonsense. I put him there myself."

"There was a body, but it wasn't his."

He took off his glasses and wiped them on his shirt. "Well, whose was it?"

"The body hasn't been identified yet." I didn't want to tell him anything more than I had to.

"What does this have to do with me?" he asked, fiddling with his pen. "If someone stole Stan's body, there is nothing I can do about it."

"How sure are you that the person you buried was Stan?"

"One hundred percent."

I moved my mouth from side to side. Sweat was beading up on Mr. Robert's forehead. I couldn't tell whether he was nervous because of the questions, or if he was hiding something.

"Is anything wrong, Mr. Roberts?"

He leaned forward, putting his elbows on the desk. "Call me Tyson. There was actually something... strange about Stan's death."

"Oh?"

"The day before he died, he had a visitor at the hospital. I was there, and Stan asked me to step in the hall so he could talk to the visitor. They had an argument. I couldn't make out what they were saying, but their voices were raised."

"Did you know the visitor?"

Tyson shook his head. "No. When the man left, I asked Stan about him. He didn't want to talk about it, and he was tired and weak, so I left him alone."

"And you didn't hear anything?"

"Nothing. I have Stan's hospital bag and some of his things in a back closet. You can look at them if you want."

"You still have them?"

"I'm not sentimental, but my sister is. She wouldn't let me throw any of it out. I'm not sure why. She never looks at it."

"Can I see it?"

"Yes, come with me." I followed him out of his office and down a short white hallway. He took out a set of keys and unlocked a storage closet. It went in about fifteen feet and was about ten feet wide with shelves on both sides. The smell of cleaning chemicals met my nose.

Tyson went inside and grabbed a backpack. He set it on one shelf and unzipped it. "There isn't anything too exciting. It has some clothing and paperwork. If I remember right, there was a watch and a notebook he liked to carry around to jot down notes."

"A notebook seems promising." I joined him in the closet and leaned in to see what the bag held. He grabbed the bag and handed it to me.

"It smells musty. It's been here for years."

I looked inside and frowned. I pulled out my phone and turned on the light. The door to the closet slammed closed, and I heard a key turn. Tyson was gone. My heart pounded, and I ran to the door and tried to turn the handle.

I smacked my hand against the solid door. It barely made a sound. "Tyson!" I yelled. "Let me out!"

On the other side of the door, I heard Tyson's voice. "Get over here now. Your mess keeps getting bigger."

I took a deep breath. Why was I so dense? My eyes scanned the closet. The walls were made of cinderblocks. I wasn't kicking my way out of here. There was no way out except the way I'd come in.

"Miss Clark? Can you hear me?" Tyson asked through the door.

"Yes! Let me out!"

"The door flew shut when I went out," he said. "It seems to be stuck. Don't worry, I called someone to come get you out."

I frowned. How stupid did he think I was? I'd heard the key in the lock. The shelves had nothing that looked useful. The door was solid. There was no way I could break it. I sat on the floor and looked through the backpack. It probably didn't even belong to Stan. It had rope, a long flashlight, a black jacket, twine, and a pair of flip-flops. I held the flashlight in my hand and moved it up and down, gauging the weight. I might be able to use it as a weapon.

There was a mop in a bucket, but the flashlight had more sustenance. I went through the shelves one by one, looking for a better weapon. When I finished, I still felt like the flashlight was my best bet.

I grabbed my phone to see what time it was, and I slapped my head with my free hand. I had my phone. It wasn't back in Tyson's office with my purse. How had I wasted time and not realized?

I dialed Jett and waited impatiently as the phone rang.

"Hey, Ivy. What's up?"

"Tyson Roberts locked me in a closet. I can't get out."

"I'm on my way. Hang up and call 911."

I hung up, but before I could call 911, I heard keys in the lock. I dropped my phone and grabbed the flashlight. Creeping to the side of the door, I held the flashlight like a sword, ready to strike.

The door opened a slit and then flew open. Tyson walked in, and I swung. I hit him in the head as hard as I could. He grabbed his head and fell to his knees. I rushed out the door and ran smack into an older man dressed all in black, and I dropped the flashlight. The man's gray hair was slicked back, and his beard hung to his chest. He grabbed my arms, and I struggled.

"STOP!" he commanded.

"I'm bleeding," Tyson said, coming out of the closet. He had a tissue pressed against his head.

"Let me go," I said.

The man sighed. "I'm afraid we can't do that."

"Why?"

"You went well beyond what I thought anyone would. Too far beyond."

"Stan Roberts?"

He nodded.

My eyes narrowed. "You aren't getting away with anything."

"Neither are you when I sue you for assault," Tyson said. "Bring her to my office. I need more tissue."

Stan half dragged me to Tyson's office. For being older, he sure was strong. When we got to the office, he pushed me into a chair and stood in front of the door. Tyson sank into his chair and grabbed a box of tissues. Stan paced in silence for what seemed like an hour, but it was probably only ten minutes. I wanted to say something but didn't know where to start.

"I've been waiting years for someone to solve the clues," Stan finally said. "I was losing hope, and then you came along. You've done remarkably well."

My eyes narrowed. "I don't understand. Why would you want someone to solve the clues if you didn't want to be found out?"

"I figured someone would come to the conclusion without digging too deep. Once you realized Jack killed Tabitha, you should have stopped. People think I'm dead, and I want it to stay that way."

"There was no evidence proving Jack did anything. Only a circled name in a book. And if you wanted me to stop, why donate that last book?"

He rubbed his chin. "What last book?"

"The one with the tomb on it. That was the reason we dug up Jack."

He blinked twice. "Dug up Jack? There was no book with a tomb."

Tyson looked up at Stan, then away.

"There was a book with a tomb on the cover that was donated to the library. It had writing on it that said, 'Justice is here.' That made me assume I needed to dig. It seemed to be the same handwriting."

"I never sent that," Stan said.

"Did you write 'Justice served' in the *No. 1 Ladies' Detective Agency*?"

"No. I only circled Jack. And what did you mean you dug up Jack?"

Tyson slammed his free hand against his desk. "Stop! Why are we talking to her? We need to get rid of her before she ruins us both!"

Stan frowned. "Get rid of her? That is out of the question. All I want from her is a promise that she won't tell anyone I'm alive."

"Did you kill Jack?" I asked Stan.

"Of course not. I'm no killer."

"Jack was buried in your grave."

Stan's eyes burned into Tyson. "What did you do?"

Tyson threw his hands into the air. "What did you expect me to do?"

My eyes narrowed. "Did you actually see Jack kill Tabitha?"

Stan nodded. "I was out on deck on one of the houseboats. I could hear them arguing. He pushed something to her face and threw her into the lake."

I glared at him. "And you just watched? You didn't yell or call for help?"

"It was too late by then. She didn't even resurface or splash around. He must have knocked her out with whatever he held to her face."

"And instead of telling anyone what you saw, you made it into a game?"

He shrugged. "Why not? It was already over."

"Then what? You killed Jack and thought that was satisfying justice?"

"I didn't kill Jack. Tyson and I went to Jack's house. I told him I knew what he did. We hoped to scare him into confessing. I had a hidden microphone so I could get him to admit it. He did, but then he tried to attack us. Tyson punched him in the face and knocked him right out. We left. A week later, I heard he had moved. I figured that meant he was going into hiding. If he's dead, this is the first I've heard of it."

I looked at the still bleeding Tyson. "You killed him and buried him in Stan's plot at the cemetery. You sent the last book. Why? What's the point in leading us directly to your crime?"

He grumbled under his breath. "I thought you would dig it up and assume it was Stan. You would think Stan killed Tabitha, and that would be the end."

Stan's brows came together. "You killed Jack?"

Tyson pointed at him. "This is all your fault. What was I supposed to do? Jack knew we were onto him, and he was a murderer. What was to keep him from killing us? I'll tell you what, nothing. I ran back in and killed him while he was knocked out."

Stan's eyes narrowed. "That's why you said you forgot something and went back in."

"I went back and cleaned up after I took you home. I shouldn't be blamed for this. Jack was a bad person. I made the world better by getting rid of him. This wouldn't have been a problem if you didn't make everything into a game."

Stan's head drooped. "You're right. I should have gone straight to the police. There is something else I might be guilty of. I'm the one who made the boat assignments. I made sure everyone on that boat hated Tabitha. She didn't deserve to have fun while people suffered because of her. I never thought anyone would kill her, but I hoped she would be so uncomfortable she would leave town."

Tyson glared at Stan. "And now we have to get rid of the girl as well."

"No," Stan said. "That isn't part of the game."

I crossed my arms. "Do you really think I'm the only one who knows all this?"

Tyson rolled his eyes. "Don't try that. You didn't know any of it until I told you."

"We were on to you, though. And I called Sheriff Malone after you locked me in the closet. He's on his way now with the entire Wichita police force." I was exaggerating, but he didn't have to know that. Jett might be the only one coming since I hadn't had time to call 911.

Tyson looked at Stan. "Now what?"

Stan opened the door. "I guess we run."

Chapter 23

Tyson and Stan ran from the building. I grabbed my purse and chased them. What I would do if I caught up to them was beyond me. I pushed through the front doors and skidded to a halt. Stan and Tyson climbed into a blue car, and the wheels squealed as they tore out of the parking lot.

Jett's truck pulled in at almost the same time. I ran over to it and jumped in the passenger seat. "Follow that car!" I exclaimed.

Jett flipped the truck around and followed the car. "How did you get away?"

"Now isn't the time! Just keep following."

Jett turned on the police siren, and the flashing red-and-blue lights began blinking from the windows. "Did you call 911?"

"No, I didn't have time."

"Call now and tell them we need backup."

"I dropped my phone. Where's yours?"

He grabbed it from his side and handed it to me. I pushed the power button and looked up at him. "What's the password?" I held on to the seat as we flew around a corner.

"Hand me the phone. I'll put in the password."

The blue car zigged in and out of traffic, but the cars were pulling over to let us through. "You can't put in your password while you're driving. Especially not in a car chase!"

I heard his teeth grind together.

"I'm not going to steal your information. If you don't trust me, you can change it later."

"It's zero, three, zero, six."

I pushed it into his phone. "That's funny. That's my birthday."

We swerved around another corner, and I dropped the phone. I think I drop phones more than the average person.

"What's your birthday?"

I leaned over and couldn't see the phone. "March sixth. It's the same as your password."

Jett's eyes didn't leave the road. "That's a weird coincidence."

I reached under the seat and grabbed the phone.

"Whoa!" Jett exclaimed, pushing on the brakes. I jerked forward. Tyson and Stan had crashed into a light pole. Jett turned off the truck and jumped out. I was right behind. Stan got out of the car and took off on foot.

"I've got him!" I yelled, sprinting after him. He looked behind him and went faster. Thankfully, there wasn't any snow or ice today, and I was making good time. He wasn't going to outrun me. I didn't look back to see whether Jett was following me or if he was getting Tyson.

"Stop, Stan!" I yelled. "Don't go down like this!"

He didn't stop, and neither did I. When I got close enough, I grabbed his jacket and jerked him backward. I felt myself falling back, and I watched Stan get flung to the side. I hit my elbows, but it wasn't bad. Stan did a roll. I popped up and ran to him before he could get up. I was ready to pounce if he tried to stand.

"Don't move," I threatened.

He rolled over on his back and looked up at the sky. He was breathing hard. "I didn't mean for Jack to get killed. I didn't even know Tyson did it."

"Running will only make you look guilty. If Tyson was the one who killed Jack, then the only thing you did was withhold evidence. It isn't a good thing, but it isn't murder. Turn yourself in."

He sat up. "I guess you're right. I shouldn't have gotten Tyson involved."

"You shouldn't have made Tabitha's death into one of your games."

"But don't you feel good about your problem-solving abilities? You solved a ten-year mystery. No one else even tried. You have to admit, it was clever."

"That doesn't make it right. Are you the one who tied up Boyd?"

His mouth turned down. "I didn't want to do that, but I had little choice. Don't hold it against me. I made sure he wasn't out there all night."

"I still don't understand. Did you stay in the woods all these years waiting for someone to come look at the grave?"

"Of course not. I lived in the woods most of the time. The trailer is mine. I made a device that would blink if anyone touched my grave. Tyson helped with it. You were the first one to do it in years. Curious people were always hanging around when it first went up, but then the excitement died down."

"The trailer wasn't Jack's?"

"No."

"Weren't you worried he would come back and wonder why you were on his land?"

He looked at the ground. "I thought he might be dead."

"I thought you said you thought he moved?"

"That's what everyone said, but I was suspicious. Tyson told me we didn't have to worry about Jack, and I didn't ask questions. I even paid the taxes on his land every year so no one would wonder. I know Jack was guilty, though. He wrote it in his journal."

"He had a journal?"

"Yes."

"Where is it?"

He raised his eyebrow. "I'm sure you'll figure it out."

I heard a siren in the distance. Jett must be with Tyson because he hadn't followed me.

Stan ran a hand over his beard. "That must be for Tyson."

"The siren?"

"He passed out while he was driving. I tried to grab the wheel, but we crashed."

I swallowed. He'd probably passed out from loss of blood. That was my fault.

"Are you ready to turn yourself in?"

He frowned. "I suppose." He got awkwardly to his feet, and we walked over to where Jett stood by Tyson's car. An ambulance and police car sped around the corner and stopped by us. Jett must have called them.

Jett's eyes widened as he looked at Stan. "Stan? You're alive?"

He looked at the ambulance. "For the most part."

"Tyson killed Jack," I told Jett. "I hit Tyson in the head with a flashlight. That's probably why he passed out and crashed. He was bleeding a lot."

Jett nodded. "Where's Boyd?"

"I couldn't find him."

"I shouldn't have had you come. We could have figured it out a different way."

A police officer got out of his car, and Jett motioned him over. I went and sat in Jett's truck and waited. I was sure someone would want to question me later, but they had a lot to think about right now. An officer placed Stan in a patrol car, and the paramedics loaded Tyson into the ambulance.

I hoped Tyson was all right. He'd done terrible things, but I didn't want to be the one who killed him. After what felt like an eternity, Jett came to the truck and got in.

"We need to go give statements at the police station."

I yawned. "I hope it doesn't take as long as the last time we did this. It must be nice to have Deputy Sheriff Ledford who can watch over things at home when you can't be there."

He let out a slow breath. "I suppose. I mean, sure, it's great to have some help, but man. That guy is critical of everything I do."

"That must be frustrating since he works under you."

"He came from Chicago and thinks we should do things like they do there. He thinks we're too backwoodsy over here. We aren't going to become friends. He's already hinted at running against me in the next election."

I frowned. "How often are elections for sheriff?"

"Every four years."

"I doubt you have to worry. He's not the most pleasant person I've ever met. I don't see him winning the hearts of the people."

"That's a hard thing to do."

"But you've done it."

"Ledford was bragging to me about getting the diner to give us free dessert. He's pretty proud of himself."

I laughed. "Did you tell him you've been getting free dessert the entire time?"

"No. Let him have that victory. I am embarrassed, though. It wasn't until he said it that I realized I always come in and eat stuff. I just walk into the kitchen like I own the place and grab any desserts you're making."

"You don't have to be embarrassed. It makes me feel good to know other people like my food."

"So tell me about today. How did you end up in a closet, and how did you escape?"

"Well, you saw Tyson's head. I bashed him with a flashlight as hard as I could. I'm still kicking myself about letting him trick me. Who goes into a close, dark space with someone they don't trust? I walked into that closet like a novice."

"It happens. So tell me about Tyson and Stan. How did Tyson get involved?"

I told him everything that had happened today and everything I'd learned. I wished I could say I'd figured the entire thing out without being told, but I hadn't. Still, the bad guys were on the way to prison... or the hospital, and this was all getting wrapped up. It could have been smoother, but I would take it as a victory.

Chapter 24

"Come see the new display," Brian said, leading me over to a book display by the front desk at the library.

I shook my head and smiled. Brian had put all the books from the case on a big stand with a poster advertising mysteries. He had the old library books that Stan had written in behind glass and new copies on small shelves so people could check them out.

"It might be weird," he said, "but ever since word got out about Stan and the books, everyone wants to check them out. I'm going to hold on to the originals."

"It's funny people want to read them. Wouldn't they want to see the clues, though?"

"I duplicated the clues in the new books. They look just like the ones Stan wrote in. I know what you're thinking.

I need to get a life. It's true, but hey. Someone has to run the library."

"It looks like you're getting ready for Christmas." Totes full of red and green decorations sat on Brian's desk.

"Yep. I usually start decorating the day after Thanksgiving, but I didn't have time until today. Are you decorating the diner?"

"I want to. I don't have any decorations, but I'll at least get a tree."

"Do you have any secret Christmas desserts that will be coming to the diner?"

I smiled mischievously. "Come on December first, and you'll see."

He grinned. "Intriguing. I'll be there."

"I better go. Creepers is with Boyd, and those two can get into trouble."

"Creepers and Boyd?"

"Yes. Boyd's trying to train him to be a police cat, but it usually ends up with Boyd stuck on the floor and Creepers scratching something up that he shouldn't."

Brian chuckled. "I've read about police cats."

I raised my eyebrow. "Police cats? Really?"

"They are usually used for pest control and stress relief."

I was still skeptical. "So the police sit around petting cats to release stress?"

"Something like that."

"I'll have to tell Boyd. Maybe we can train Creepers to sit on Jett's lap and help him with his stress."

"That shouldn't be hard."

My eyes lit up. "Maybe we should get him a cat."

Brian smiled. "I tried. The litter Creepers came from had six kittens. I offered one to him, but he said no. He's more of a dog person."

"Does he have a dog?"

"No, but he did when he was younger. He was pretty traumatized when she died. His parents didn't want to get another one since it upset him so much."

"How long ago was that?"

Brian scratched his head. "Hmm. I can't remember exactly, but he was in high school."

"Dogs are fun, but I don't think I could manage one at the diner. Creepers already thinks he owns the place."

"He gets off the windowsill now?"

"A lot more than he did at first. I always hear about feisty kittens, but he's always seemed so mellow compared to others I've seen."

"He was calm when I had him."

"He's begun to run around the diner more. I keep expecting complaints about him being there, but you were right. No one seems to care."

"Everyone knows the mice are bad around here. They all understand."

"I am glad you gave him to me. He's a sweetheart." I looked at my phone. "I better get going. Thanks for all your help with the case. I never would have figured some of it out without you."

"Sure. It was interesting."

I said goodbye and walked back to the diner. I went inside and found it full.

Livy passed me on her way to a table. "Go see what Boyd's doing in the kitchen," she said as she walked by.

I rushed into the kitchen to find Boyd with Creepers. Creepers was wearing a harness and leash and was walking around with Boyd.

"How did you get him to cooperate?" I asked.

Boyd's grin spread across his face. "I've been working on it whenever you aren't around. I think he's beginning to like it. By spring, I bet you'll be able to take him on walks."

I bent down and rubbed his head. "That will be fun, won't it?" He meowed and pressed his head into my hand.

Livy poked her head in. "Hey, guys. Good news and bad news. Jett's here."

José turned from the skillet. "And the bad news?"

"He's with Deputy Sheriff Ledford."

All the cooks moaned, and my brows came together. "I take it you've all met the deputy?"

Anton turned from where he was frying a batch of tater tots. "Oh, we've all met him."

Carrie leaned against the island and folded her arms. "He came in the kitchen last night so we would all recognize him. He wanted us to all know what he looked like so he could get his free desserts."

"I think he's tried all of them," José said.

"I can go take their order," I said. "He probably won't be as bad with Jett." I grabbed a notepad and made my way out of the kitchen and over to the table where Jett and Deputy Sheriff Ledford were sitting.

"Hello." I greeted them with a smile.

Jett smiled back. The deputy looked neutral.

"What can I get you two?"

Jett shrugged. "Tell José to send out whatever he thinks is best today."

I tilted my head. "That could be dangerous. You never know what that might be."

His mouth turned up. "I'm feeling adventurous."

"Alright. And how about you?" I didn't want to spout off the man's full title.

He glanced at the menu and smirked. "I'll have a piece of apple pie, a cinnamon roll, and water."

I refused to react. If he only ate desserts, that was fine by me. He would be the one with a stomachache. He probably thought he was gaming the system.

"I just got a call from Wichita."

I looked up from my pad. "Oh yeah?"

"Stan is sticking with his story. He says he has Jack's journal somewhere but won't say where. He said it's safe to say that the diner girl will get the picture and figure it out."

I rolled my eyes. "Diner girl? He didn't give any clues about where it was. Have you checked his trailer yet?"

"No. It's all confusing. The trailer belongs to Stan, but the property belonged to Jack. Now that Jack is dead and has no family, there is some uncertainty about what to do."

Ledford sighed. "You shouldn't be discussing this with her."

"I'll go get your food," I told them. "Do you want any dessert, Jett?"

He ran a hand through his hair and shook his head. "I'm trying to cut back."

"You should address him as Sheriff Malone." Ledford narrowed his eyes.

Jett grabbed my hand and ran his thumb over it. "It's alright, Ledford. Ivy and I are on a first-name basis."

"Your food will be out in a few minutes." I pulled away and turned, hoping Ledford didn't see my pink cheeks. I took a few steps, then I froze. Could it be that simple? Stan said, "It's safe to say..." What if there was a safe in the trailer? The numbers in the books—12, 7, 32—could be the combination.

"Ivy?" Jett said. "Is everything okay?"

I spun around. "Did Stan use the exact words 'it's safe to say' or was it just something similar?"

"That's what he said."

"I bet there's a safe in the trailer, and I bet the numbers written in the books are the combination. And if he said I would 'get the picture,' I bet it's behind a picture!"

Ledford shook his head. "That's the silliest thing I've ever heard. I think you've seen too many movies."

Jett stood. "No, I think she might be right. I don't think Stan thought he would ever be caught, but he wanted someone to find the evidence."

Ledford stood, and for the first time, I realized he was only about an inch taller than my five foot five inches. "Don't get overexcited. We don't have a warrant."

Jett pulled out his cell phone. "No, but I bet I can make a few calls and get Stan to give us permission to go through his things."

"I'll grab my coat," I said, turning to leave.

"What about my food?" Ledford asked.

I looked over my shoulder as I walked away. "I'll have it sent out." My coat was on a hook by the back door. I grabbed it and turned to José. "José, I think I know where Jack's journal is. I'll be back soon."

"Be careful."

"I'm going with Jett." I rushed out, hoping it was true. Jett hadn't said he was going, only that he was making a few calls. He and Ledford appeared to be arguing from their booth. Jett glanced at me, and I pointed outside. He nodded, and I went out into the frosty fall air.

This was what we needed to have everything wrapped up. If Jack really had written a confession, then we would know that Tabitha had been killed, and it wasn't an accident. Right now, everything was going on the assumption it had happened because Stan said so. It wasn't a convincing argument.

Chapter 25

Jett came outside, and we climbed into his truck. It felt like it had taken him forever, but that could be because it was so cold.

"We have permission to go in the trailer. Stan is being cooperative, but I think he wants us to find the journal, so it isn't surprising. The trailer will be moved since Stan shouldn't have put it there in the first place."

"Your partner didn't want to come?"

Jett rolled his eyes. "He says he'll meet me later. He needs to eat his dessert."

"It sounds like he really wants to get his free food. My staff said he's tried just about every dessert we offer."

"I want to mock him for that, but I'm sure I've had multiple of everything in the diner. I didn't realize how much free food you let me eat until Ledford came. Don't worry, I will be paying for everything I eat. Sorry about before. I don't know why I never thought about it."

"It's not the same. Giving away free desserts every day doesn't hurt my costs. You're a friend, so I'm happy to give them to you. Ledford is demanding, which makes the staff resentful. You've never demanded free things."

Jett started the truck and pulled out. "No, but I came into the kitchen and ate it without even thinking."

"It's still not the same. Everyone at the diner respects you and likes you. If Ledford had been pleasant in any way, no one would have cared. I have a feeling he'll be more of an obstacle to you than helpful."

"I have the same feeling."

We drove the rest of the way in silence. I hoped my guess was right. We pulled into the cemetery parking lot, and I got out of the truck and walked to Jett's side. He opened his door and got out.

"This will be a new experience for you." He grinned.

I cocked my head. "What are you talking about?"

"Going into the woods when it isn't dark."

I smiled. "That will be nice."

Getting to the trailer felt faster than the last time. Probably because it was light, and I wasn't worried about anyone popping out and trying to stop us. In the light, the trailer didn't look spooky at all. It had white vinyl panels and a bright blue door.

Jett climbed the two steps to the door and tried the knob. It turned easily, and we entered.

"I was hoping you'd have to bust down the door," I joked. "Walking right in is anticlimactic."

Jett knocked his fist against the door. It sounded hollow. "It wouldn't have been hard to bust through. I bet Boyd could even do it."

I looked around the neat front room. Stan had been organized. A leather sofa faced a TV with a dark wooden coffee table in front of it. Five framed paintings hung on the walls.

"Boyd could even do it?" I asked. "Are you putting down old people?"

He chuckled. "I was going to say you could even do it, but then you would have asked if I said it because you're a girl."

I grinned as I walked toward a painting. "Probably. You can't insult me, though. I saved us last month."

"Yes, you did," Jett said, pulling a painting away from the wall. "And I appreciate it."

I peeked behind a painting of mountains, but there was nothing. We checked all the paintings in the room, then moved down the hall. There was a bedroom with no paintings and then an office.

"That has to be it," I said, pointing at a painting of a barn on the wall behind a large oak desk. We bolted around the desk, and I watched expectantly as Jett removed the picture. A black safe appeared behind the painting.

Jett placed the painting on the floor and smiled at me. "You were right."

My smile was so big it hurt. "And Ledford was right. It is like a movie, and that makes it even more exciting."

"What was the combination?"

"It's 12, 7, 32. Hopefully, in that order."

Jett fiddled with the lock, and I heard a click. The safe opened, and I held in a squeal. Jett pulled out a black leather-bound journal and handed it to me.

I opened it, ready to flip to the last page, but there was only writing on the first one. "Tabitha Coats was the biggest mistake of my life," I read out loud. "I never should have dated her, and I never should have fallen for her garbage. I lost twenty-five thousand dollars investing with her, and she seemed to think that was no big deal. Did I throw her in the lake? Yes. Am I sorry? Not at all. She got what she deserved, and I bet a large portion of the population in Muddy Creek agrees with me. I'm leaving this for someone to find. I found a lot of money at Tabitha's, and with luck, I'll be so far gone by that point that no one around here will ever see me again. Don't even try looking. By the time you do, I'll be in a different country. Jack McBride."

"Well, that settles it in my mind," Jett said. "Of course we'll have to have a professional go over it to make sure Jack wrote it."

I handed it back to him. "It's funny he thinks she deserved it for taking people's money, but then he took the money she stole from other people. I wonder where the money ended up."

"I bet Tyson took it. When I was talking to an officer on the phone today, he said Tyson had a large sum of money dropped into his account eight years ago. They weren't sure what it meant, and he wasn't talking."

"So now what?"

"Now we're done. Well, we might need to testify, but I think that's about it. Now, what are you going to do with your spare time?"

I laughed. "What do you mean spare time? I promised Barbra I would get her house under control, and that will take forever. Between that and the diner renovations, I should keep pretty busy."

"Right, Barbra. Let me know if you ever need my truck. With your luck, you'll find a body in there and turn it into a mystery."

I shook my head. "Not at Barbra's… although she has this humongous wardrobe at her house. She got it from an estate sale or something like that."

"I helped her bring that in."

"Right, she said that. Well, it's packed full of stuff, and I can't wait to go through it. I can't believe Barbra hasn't looked through it. There could be anything."

"Probably just a bunch of junk."

"Maybe, but I'm excited to see inside."

He nodded. "I'll take you back to the diner, then I need to get this journal to Wichita." We walked back to the truck, and my mouth turned down when I saw a silver car pull in next to us. Jett let out a slow breath. "That's Ledford."

Ledford got out of the car and spotted the journal in Jett's hand. "You actually found it?"

"Yep," Jett said. "It was right where Ivy thought it would be. I'm going to take it to Wichita."

He crossed his arms. "I'll hold things together here."

"Thanks."

Chapter 26

Barbra sat on her sofa in her front room with Creepers on her lap. I'd cleared away enough stuff to make a path to the sofa, and I'd vacuumed it and sprayed something on it to make it smell less musty.

"So everything is getting tied up about Tabitha?" Barbra asked.

I popped open a box. "It looks like it. Jett thinks Tyson and possibly Stan will end up in prison."

"Tyson is Stan's cousin?"

"Yes." I could hear Creepers purring from her lap.

"Why Stan?" she asked. "The cousin I understand, but Stan didn't do anything."

"For withholding evidence. He'd known what happened to Tabitha for years and didn't tell anyone. He also suspected Jack was dead."

"Stan and his silly games. No one would have ever looked into it if you hadn't been around. I can't believe what that man will go through just to make up a puzzle. It's not new either. He was like that as a little boy even. They had to ban hide-and-seek when he was young because he would hide really well and refuse to come out until someone found him. He hid for five hours one time. His poor mother was so stressed."

"I can imagine. I'm just glad I didn't kill Tyson. The flashlight was bulky, and I hit him really hard. When he passed out, I was really worried, but they said he's fine."

"He got less than he deserved."

"Do you scrapbook?" I asked, holding up a few packages of colorful paper.

"No. I thought I might get into it, but I never did."

I looked into the box. It was packed with stickers and stencils. "This stuff still looks good. Do you think you'll ever use it?"

"I want to say yes, but I know it's a lie. We should give it to Opal. She loves scrapbooking. That's why I started getting things. We thought it would be fun to do together, but I always had an excuse to avoid it."

"Alright, I'll drop it off for her when I leave." I peered over at the wardrobe. It would still take a while before we could get to it. If I came over every day for a week or two, we might be there.

Barbra's eyes sparkled. "I'm impressed by your patience. I see you looking at that wardrobe every five minutes. We could just push everything out of the way and start cleaning it out."

I shook my head. "Waiting gives me more motivation."

She raised her brow. "Come on. You are going to die of curiosity if we don't look."

"Come on, Barbra. Don't tempt me."

"No, it's decided," she said. "We are going through it today." She put Creepers on the chair and started pushing boxes to the side.

"Stop, you don't want to hurt yourself. We have plenty of time."

"I'm an old woman. Time is not something I have to waste."

"You've had that thing for years, and you've never gone through it. Waiting another week or two won't hurt."

She grinned. "I'm going to open it whether or not you help."

My shoulders drooped. She probably wouldn't really open it without me, but I wanted to be here when it happened. "Fine," I grumbled, grabbing a box and moving it to the side.

She laughed and pulled her hair back into a ponytail. "Don't pretend you don't want to."

"Tell me more about the Clements," I said, putting one box on another. "It seems strange they would live out here and not interact with anyone in the town."

"I think having too much money does weird things to people. They think the things they do are more impressive than things anyone else does. The Clements are from old money, so none of them have had to work a day in their lives. They own a company, but from what I understand, they hire people to run it."

"Why don't they go live in a place with people like them?"

"I'm not sure. Maybe they like to be the mysterious people living out in the middle of nowhere. It's possible they enjoy knowing the people in Muddy Creek are gossiping about them and making up whatever we want to."

"Have you ever met any of them?"

"No. Even when I went to the big sale at their house, none of them were visible."

I tried to pick up a tote, but it was too heavy, so I slid it to the side. "You told me before that they like to have parties. I wonder what they're like."

"I've never heard of anyone who was invited."

"Do they have kids? Surely they go to school?"

Barbra picked up a small box. "None of them have young kids. Zeb Clements was the man who died. He was the grandfather. He had two children, but they are both in their upper sixties. They had private schooling. Both of them are married. Their son has two children, and their daughter has one. Those children are in their forties. The families all live together in Clements Manor."

"And the grandchildren of Zeb Clements don't have children?"

"No one around here knows. What I've told you is as far as the Muddy Creek gossip goes. I've never met a single person who knows them."

"What if they don't really exist?" I joked.

She laughed. "The Clements have always been the talk of the town. Since no one knows them, the stories can get pretty strange."

I pushed the last few boxes to the side and put my hand to my stomach. This was it.

"I'm afraid you'll be disappointed when all we find is some old trousers."

I giggled. "I probably will. It's still exciting."

"You should go to storage shed sales."

"What's that?"

"You know the storage sheds people rent to store their junk in?"

"Yes."

"Well, sometimes people never come back to claim their stuff and stop paying their bills. When that happens, they have a big sale, and you can bid on people's things. Then you clean them out and get whatever you find."

"Is that how you ended up with so much stuff?"

Her eyes twinkled. "Partially."

"That actually sounds really fun. Maybe we could do that when we're done decluttering your house."

"So we could fill it up again?"

I laughed. "No, just for fun. We could have a huge sale after we went through all the stuff."

"I'm up for it."

My phone rang, and I pulled it out of my pocket. "It's José."

"Go ahead and take it."

I pressed the button. "Hey, José."

"Ivy, one of the ovens isn't working, and Anton had to go home sick. Do you think you can come help?"

I glanced at the wardrobe. It would have to wait. "Sure, I'll be right over."

"Thanks."

I hung up. "They need me at the diner. Will you wait to open it until I come back?"

Barbra smiled. "Of course I will. I've put it off for this long."

"Thanks, you're the best."

I grabbed the box of scrapbooking supplies and left. I dropped them at Opal's house before I went to the diner. The diner parking was full, and I had to circle the block. When I got inside, my eyes ran across the tables. They were almost all full. I was glad I'd decided to expand.

I rushed into the kitchen to see all the cooks hard at work. I washed my hands, threw on an apron and hairnet, and got to work.

"Sorry to call you in like this," José said. "I thought of asking Boyd, but it's cold today, and he would have to ride his bike."

"It's not a problem. What's wrong with the oven?"

"I'm not sure. We might need to call a repair company."

I could hear hammers out back. It took all my self-control not to check on the expansion progress every few minutes. These workers were fast. They had already put down the foundation and were starting to frame.

"What do you need me to do?"

"We're out of brownies, and the book club is coming in tonight."

"I'm on it." I plugged in the mixer. The book club met at the diner once a month, and last month, we had made over seventy dollars from the brownies and cookies they ordered.

The kitchen door swung open, and Jett and Boyd entered. "Ivy, how are things?" Jett asked.

"Good. What's going on?"

"I just got a call from Wichita. They are positive that Jack wrote the journal entry. You should get a medal for most cases solved in a year."

I waved my hand in dismissal. "I didn't do that great of a job. It was all a little messy."

"Most things are. You did great. You too, José and Boyd."

José shrugged. "I'll be more useful when I retire someday. I missed a bunch of stuff."

"We missed out on catching the bad guys," Boyd said. "You should have taken me with you."

I scooped some sugar from a container. "I was going to, but I couldn't find you."

Boyd's mouth turned down. "The one time I go to a movie, everything happens."

"Well, I'm glad to have it all out in the open," Jett said. "Now I can go back to some things I've been working on without feeling guilty."

"What type of things?" José asked.

"Just the normal stuff. I've been putting off a lot of paperwork. With luck, Ivy won't find any dead bodies or clues or anything else for a month or two. Then I might get caught up."

I smiled. "I've already decided on my next project."

Jett groaned. "I hope it's a cross-stitch."

Everyone laughed.

"No, I'm going to go through Zeb Clements's wardrobe."

Boyd chuckled. "That's the oddest thing I've ever heard. Why would you want to do that?"

"Barbra bought it a few years ago but never went through it. Anything could be inside."

"As long as it's not a dead body, I'm all for it," Jett said. "And take all the time you need."

"If any of you want to help, you are welcome. Well, if Barbra agrees. Don't you think it would be interesting? It could have anything."

"I'll pass on sorting Zeb's old boxers," José said.

"Me too," Boyd said. "Unless of course there really is a body in there, then I'm in."

"There isn't going to be a body," I said. "Just think of what could be in it, though. It might be interesting."

Boyd shook his head. "Or be a waste of time."

"Maybe, but I still think it will be fun. If none of you are going to help, I could ask Brian. I bet he likes things like that."

"Probably," Boyd said. "Brian is a history nerd, so he would probably enjoy it."

Jett shook his head. "Don't take Brian. He's probably busy."

I raised my eyebrow, and Boyd snorted. Why would Brian be busy? The library wasn't a happening place.

José filled a plate with salad. "Just don't go talking to the Clements family. They value their privacy."

"Why would I go talk to them?"

"I don't know. I can imagine you finding something and wanting the backstory. I don't think they would be happy about that."

"Don't worry. I don't plan on it."

Jett looked into my mixing bowl. "What are you making?"

"Brownies."

"I wish I could stay around and get one, but I have a lot to do. I might drop by later and get one to go. Ledford and I have a long night of paperwork ahead of us."

"Are you allowed to call him Ledford?" Carrie asked from her place at the stove. "I called him Deputy Ledford, and I got a five-minute lecture on how to address him properly."

Jett grinned. "He stopped lecturing me after the third time. I think he's realized I'm not going to say Deputy Sheriff Ledford sixty times a day."

"I heard he might run against you next election," José said.

Jett nodded. "He's welcome to. I don't see him as much of a threat. He hasn't endeared himself to the town thus far."

I tuned them all out when they started talking about politics. I should be taking the time to relax with a book, but all I could think about was Zeb Clements's wardrobe and all the possible secrets it could be hiding. Boyd could be right, and it might be full of clothes, but I was hoping for more. Not a secret like Stan Roberts had been keeping, but perhaps a family secret of some sort. I knew it was unlikely, but life was more fun when you expected something out of the ordinary.

Chocolate Zucchini Brownies

1/2 cup vegetable oil

1 1/2 cups granulated sugar

1 tbsp vanilla

2 cups all-purpose flour

1/2 cup unsweetened cocoa powder

1 tsp salt

3 cups shredded zucchini

1 1/2 - 2 cups chocolate chips

Preheat oven to 350 degrees. Combine oil, sugar, and vanilla. Add flour, cocoa, salt, and baking soda. Mix. Stir in zucchini. **Do not** drain it first. Let rest for five to ten minutes. Add in chocolate chips and stir. Spread mixture into a sprayed 9x13 pan and bake for 23-30 minutes. Test with a toothpick.

About the Author

Kristy Dixon received a degree in English from the University of Utah. She started writing stories when she was seven and never stopped. She enjoys writing fantasy books for middle grade and teens and cozy mysteries. At home, she spends her time playing board games with her husband and kids and writing. Occasionally she takes part in a Super Mario marathon. She has six chickens and a cat that help keep life amusing. If she isn't playing with her kids or writing, she is usually eating cookies, or wishing she was eating cookies.

Also By Kristy Dixon

www.ingramcontent.com/pod-product-compliance
Lightning Source LLC
Chambersburg PA
CBHW030540170626
46820CB00036B/900

* 9 7 8 1 9 6 0 8 4 1 2 6 1 *